Lying Lanier

An Eva St. Claire Mystery

By M.K. Stabley

Lying Lanier
by M.K. Stabley

First Edition August 2021

Cover Artwork by Canva and
M.K. Stabley

Dedication

This book is dedicated to my family and friends, for their continued support, encouragement and love that they've given me over the years. I can't thank you all enough.

Kris, Hunter, Mom and Dad W, Mom and Dad S, Kim D, Karen H, Karen N, Gail W, Christie M, Perrie P, Anne M, Tricia R, Dara M, Debbie B, Teresa M, Chris R, Laurie F, Debbie K, Kristen T, Lara G, Kara SB, Sandy T, MaryRose F, Katrin T, Amy W, and if I forgot anyone, I am so sorry.

I love you all, so much!

Table of Contents

Table of Contents continued

Prologue

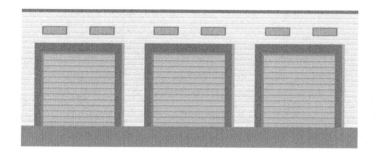

Kris watched as Eva punched the code into the security door and the light flashed green. She rolled the narrow door of the 11x12 storage unit up, showing an empty, dark space in front of them. It was the most basic unit she could find. They didn't want to spend a ton of money.

"Well, this is it. It looks big enough for the safe, right?"

Kris looked inside, mentally calculating the dimensions. "Yeah, the safe should fit through this door. I wasn't sure the opening would be tall enough, but it looks like it will just fit."

They backed out of the unit and walked the short distance to the small U haul truck they rented for the day.

Kris opened the back door revealing the 10x3 black steel fire/gun safe that now housed the Pewag chain and padlock clad box, which contained the demonic spirits of Dagon and Lilith. The 10 gauge steel walled door and frame of the safe should be more than proficient enough to contain the box, but they weren't taking any chances, hence the chain and padlock wrapped around it.

Eva climbed onto the back of the truck and grabbed the hand-truck, while Kris adjusted the ramp, so they could roll it down and into the unit, without breaking their backs.

After rolling the safe to the far end of the storage unit, Eva looked over at Kris, "do you think this will work? Maybe I should have taken it back to Connecticut, to my family's property and buried it right where the Dagon had come out."

"No, this place is fine; it's more than secure. For god sake, I've wrapped and double wrapped the chest in chains that are virtually impenetrable and a padlock, as well as placing it in that steel safe."

"Okay, I trust your judgment. And frankly, I just want this part of our lives to be over and put behind us. We've been back from Kentucky for a month now and I haven't had any dreams with my mother in them, so that has to mean something, right?"

Kris slung his arm around her shoulder and gave her a squeeze, "I'm glad you trust my judgment, but all of that aside, I'm relieved that your dreams have subsided, and I hope it stays that way. Hopefully we can get back to our normal boring lives. Who knew boring would sound so good."

"I agree, boring sounds like heaven. Let's lock this baby up and get out of here."

"I'm right behind you."

Just as Kris was closing the bay door to the U haul, his phone went off, alerting him to a text. He shut the door, locked it, and pulled out his phone to check the message, "You have got to be kidding me."

Kris, it's Jake. How soon do you think you and Eva could get to Atlanta, GA?

Kris shook his head and opened the drivers side of the truck, mumbling under his breath as he positioned himself in the truck.

"What's wrong? Why are you swearing under your breath?"

"We need to get the truck back and get home, so I can make reservations for us to fly to Atlanta. I'm going to call my Mom real quick to see if she minds coming over to stay with the kids."

Eva froze, her mouth set in a frown, "Jake messaged you, I assume?"

"That he did. You are needed in Atlanta, Georgia, as soon as I can get you there."

"Well, crap on a cracker. He said there would always be a next time."

Chapter One

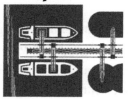

Marcella Gallo started making her rounds at Atlantic Sea, Inc. before heading home for the night. She walked into the plant, which was dark, except for a small slice of light inside one of the boats. That's when she noticed a man sitting in one of the cigarette boats on the opposite side of the plant that was set to be transported to South America this week

.

She didn't recognize the man as anyone who worked for Atlantic Sea, Inc., so she backed herself into the shadows and observed him for a minute.

The vantage point from where she was at wasn't great, but she could see that the steering column had been taken off, that much was evident. Marcella pulled out her phone, swiped for her camera, and zoomed in to get a closer look at the man, and to see what he was doing. Her mouth dropped open and she started snapping pictures.

Her phone dinged with a notification, and she fumbled with it, nearly dropping it before she regained control. The volume on her phone hadn't been on silent, but she wasn't exactly expecting to find what she was currently observing either. Luckily where she was hiding, it was exceptionally dark.

The man she was taking pictures of heard the slight noise in the distance and his head jerked up in her direction. Marcella was sure he couldn't see her from all the tall machinery, shelves, and the lack of light, but she crouched down anyway, and made her way to the exit. She was crawling on her hands and knees faster than she'd ever moved before. Once she was outside the plant entrance, she ran to her office, grabbing her purse and keys and high-tailed it out of there, before he caught her.

She made it to her car in the parking lot and was thankful that her car wasn't the only one still there.

Marcella pulled her phone out and looked over all the pictures she had been able to get, and still couldn't believe what she saw. The steering column had definitely been taken off, and small bags filled with a white powdery substance was inside. It didn't take a Rocket Scientist to figure out what it was, but why or who the man was behind the whole thing, was another story.

As she pushed the button to start her car, she decided that she would go to Alec tomorrow, first thing.

Alec Brighton, CEO of Atlantic Sea, Inc., probably had no clue that someone in his organization let this guy in and was contaminating their boats and using them as drug mules, so to speak.

Marcella took one last look around the parking lot, then toward the front door, making sure it was clear before she took off. Her nerves were frazzled, but she was bound to get to the bottom of this, tomorrow morning.

Chapter Two

Jose knew he heard the sound of a phone notification off in the distance, and knew it wasn't his phone that made the noise. Someone was here, who wasn't supposed to be. Scanning the area, nothing stood out, but it was dark, except for the pen light he was using. He figured it could have come from out in the hall, if there were some stragglers still working.

He didn't have time to think about it too much, because he had to get the steering column reconnected on this boat, so he could move on to the next two and get the heck out of there.

Jose was the middle man, the mechanic. He knew how to disassemble the steering columns, place the goods inside and put everything back together, and no one was the wiser. It had been that way for the last twenty years. His job was an easy one, but it required a skill not many people had.

Jose Vergara, forty-seven years old, and a transplant from Juarez, Mexico, was blackmailed into doing this job by Diego Martinez, the Drug Kingpin of Georgia and Florida. Martinez has ties to the Mexican Cartel and with some of Jose's family still living in Juarez, he didn't really have a choice. Diego always hung his family over his head, because he knew that would be his achilles heel... his kryptonite. So, he did what he had to do and left. Every now and then he'd take care of a problem if it arose, but they were far and few between.

Luckily his wife and kids never knew what he did on the side. They only knew the man he wanted to be, and the one he led them to think he was; owner of a successful auto body shop, north of Atlanta and a junk yard that was located south of the city..

As Jose was finishing with the last boat, he still had a nagging feeling in the pit of his stomach that wouldn't go away. Did someone see him; see what he put into the steering columns? He had never had this feeling before, while working on the boats. It had to have been that phone notification he heard off in the distance. It was making him paranoid.

"Great, now I'm getting as paranoid as those junkies who smoke and inject this crap."

He gathered up his small tool belt, double and triple checking that every tool he brought with him was accounted for, continued to keep his latex gloves on, making sure he didn't leave any prints that would incriminate him later.

Jose jumped down off the boat, and made his way to the side entrance of the plant that he had come in at, took the key that was given to him and locked the door.

His late model car was parked a street over, in the Industrial Park that Atlantic Sea, Inc. was located in. He never parked in the actual business parking lot. He took a lot of precautions where this job was concerned. He could never get caught. That was his number one priority.

Jose got to his car, angled himself in and stripped his hands of the gloves. He stretched his fingers outward and held them up to the vents where the air cooled his sweating palms.

"I don't know how many more times I can do this job," he said to himself.

Just as he was about to pull out and head home, his phone vibrated. A text from his wife, *"Are you still at work? When will you be home?"*

He put the car back into park, and responded to her. He hated lying to her, but it was for his family's safety.

"Just leaving, be home soon. Love you."

Chapter Three

Marcella was sitting on her black leather couch in the great room of her one story lake house that overlooks Lake Lanier, watching television, when she grabbed her phone and looked over the pictures she took at the plant.

Marcella Gallo, no relation to Ernest and Julio, is the office manager and executive assistant to the CEO of Atlantic Sea, Inc. She is your a-typical workaholic. Her job means everything to her. It's one of the reasons she still remains single. To her, relationships just get in the way of becoming more successful. She's tried doing both, but the job always wins out. It's not as if she can't get a date, she is five foot seven, with an athletic build, long wavy chestnut brown hair, chocolate lava eyes, and beautiful olive skin, all of which she inherited from her Italian heritage. She dresses in the newest haute couture from Neiman Marcus or Bloomingdales. Her go to power outfit is her black Christian Louboutin heels, with her signature gray houndstooth patterned Saint Laurent pantsuit. The pantsuits are more her style than the traditional skirt and blouse, due in part to her thinking that she gets taken more seriously in the pantsuit, than in the latter.

She continued to obsess over the pictures and zoomed in on one of them, studying the man sitting in the boat, obviously planting drugs into the steering column. She was trying to place him, but Marcella didn't recognize the man at all, and she knew every person that worked at Atlantic Sea, whether they worked in the offices, the plant or on the shipping docks. She made it one of her priorities to know every employee. It was one of the things that made her good at her job. But this man was an enigma to her, and she didn't like it.

She immediately sent a text to her boss, Alec Brighton, saying that she needed to speak to him first thing tomorrow morning.

Marcella got up from the couch, heading into the kitchen to grab a glass of wine, when her phone dinged with an incoming message. She assumed it was Alec, so she continued to pour her glass of wine and took it back to the couch. Settling in, she opened her phone and swiped to see messages, but it wasn't Alec, it was from the last guy she had gone out with, a month ago.

"Some guys just can't take no for an answer," she said to herself out loud.

She wasn't even going to message him back. Once Marcella broke it off with someone, it was a done deal.

By 11:30, she still hadn't heard anything back from Alec, so she retreated to her bedroom, to try to get some sleep.

It was a futile attempt and she knew it. She tossed and turned every ten minutes. Worry had her stomach tied in knots. Who in the organization could be the drug dealer? Marcella lay awake picturing every employee and their background, and couldn't come up with a viable suspect.

She personally did all the background checks on everyone that worked for Atlantic Sea, Inc.

"Well, everyone except...no, can't be.

Chapter Four

Alec Brighton was pacing the floor in front of the wall of windows that faced out at the great expanse of Lake Lanier, from his four thousand square foot contemporary style lake house after receiving a text from his second in charge, Marcella. She hadn't expanded on why she needed to talk to him first thing tomorrow morning, and if truth be told, he was more than a little on edge.

Alec knew Diego's guy was going to be doing his thing tonight after everyone left. This happened like clockwork, every two months, and every two months he would constantly be on alert, wondering if anyone suspected what he was part of. And until those boats left the warehouse in a couple days, he would stay vigilant and nervous. Lucky for him, he had something he could take, to take the edge off.

He wasn't a druggy by any sense of the word, but he would sample the product that was to be going out every shipment. He never let himself get strung out or anything. Once it left his warehouse though, he didn't care who took it from there.

Mr. Martinez had a man that worked at the Port Authority in Savannah, Georgia and one that worked at the Customs and Port Authority in Cartagena, Columbia in South America. It's been a three-year partnership, so far, and the money was worth it. Not that Alec was hurting for money, he was one of the biggest manufacturers of the "cigarette boat" in the country.

The Cigarette boat got its name from Donald Aronow, who built the first one back in the 1960s. His reasoning for the name was because of its long, sleek look that resembled a cigarette.

Back then the cost for one was 450k, now they run over Two Million dollars. The price is high, but that particular boat is typically fifty-five feet in length, has three cabins, with the Master having its own private bath, along with a guest state room and a smaller single berth cabin.

The speed on a cigarette boat tops out at 92 mph, and it has six Mercury Racing 450 R V-8 outboard engines, which produce 450HP (horse power), which gives the boat a total of 2400 HP. This type of boat is definitely not for the average fisherman. Typically big celebrities, like rappers, athletes, and well, drug runners, to name a few are the ones who purchase such a boat. And those who are avid racers, in that category.

Alec headed for his personal gym that he had built after purchasing the house. He took his stress out on the dumbbells and his boxing bag. Alec's in his mid forties, young-looking, and keeps fit. He stands over six foot, with a lean, but muscular body. People always assume he is much younger. He kept his sandy blond hair cropped short and stylish, and was currently sporting three days worth of beard growth. He spends virtually every weekend on the lake, so he was pretty tan, which concealed his English ancestry.

While delivering a few right hooks and an uppercut to the heavy bag, Alec's phone pinged again. "Now what?"

Alec bent down to retrieve his phone from the weight bench and read the text.

"It's finished."

He let out a long breath that he'd been holding in, and gave the heavy bag a hard jab, before heading back upstairs to relax.

Chapter Five

Marcella arrived at the Atlantic Sea, Inc. office before 7am. She wanted to be there before Alec, so she could talk to him as soon as he got there. She was exhausted, and needed coffee. Sleep had eluded her last night after she had the thought that Alec could be the one that is mixed up in the whole drug shipping thing.

Marcella made up her mind that morning, while staring at the ceiling, that if he is in fact part of this, she would quit on the spot. She would not work for someone involved in illegal activity, no matter how much she loved her job.

The noise from the elevator doors opening startled her out of her thoughts. "Oh crap, he's here," she said. "Okay, let's get this over with. It may be a short day," she whispered to herself as she walked out of her office.

Marcella came around the corner just as Alec was exiting the elevator. He looked up and gasped,

"Jeez Mar, you scared the crap out of me. What are you doing here so early," he asked.

"Didn't you get my text last night? We need to talk now."

"I did, but I didn't realize it was that important, let's go to my office."

Marcella followed him to his office. Alec's office was large and said "in charge", with floor to ceiling windows that ran at least fifty feet across and sixteen feet in height. His 80" light gray oak table/desk was positioned in the center of the room, flanked by four oak bookcases on the back wall that matched the desk, a bar set up on the right wall and a coffee colored leather sofa was against the far wall. There are two club chairs placed in front of his desk, for visitors and clients, and the lighting fixture that hung above his desk was a farmhouse wood chandelier with four Edison lights. The paint color on the walls is a dark iron ore. Manly is an understatement here. Marcella loved the decor in Alec's office. Her office is pretty understated compared to his.

Alec sat in his wing back chair behind his desk, his elbows resting on his desk, with his fingers steepled, looking serious, and maybe a little anxious.

"What's up Marcella?"

She angled herself around to one of the club chairs and perched herself on the edge, her phone in hand and internally shaking like a leaf.

"I was here last night, pretty late and I always try to check everything before I leave, for security reasons. Well, when I opened the door to the plant I noticed someone was sitting in one of the boats that is supposed to go out this week."

Marcella stopped briefly to see if there would be any reaction from Alec. She noticed a slight twitch, but nothing else, so she continued.

"The steering wheel of the boat had been removed, and the man was fiddling with something, so I got my phone out and took a few pictures." That got a reaction.

"I see. May I see the pictures you took?"

She pulled up the pictures on her phone to show him. Marcella was glad she decided to send them to her email, as well as her friend's email, too, before showing him. Her mind was reeling. If he is a part of this, he may delete the pictures. She patted herself on the back for thinking ahead.

Alec swiped through the pictures, one after the other. His face showed very little effect.

"I appreciate you bringing this to my attention and I'll be dealing with it from here on out. Can you send these to my phone?

"Of course. Are you going to call the police? You definitely don't want Atlantic Sea, Inc. involved in a drug scandal, right Alec?"

"I will take care of this, you just go back to doing your job, deal?"

"You're going to call the authorities, right?" Marcella was pushing the envelope, and she knew it. But, if he wasn't going to stop the drug running, then she would.

"I said I would handle it, Marcella, end of discussion."

She got up to leave, turned around and cleared her throat, "if you don't stop this, then I will be forced to quit and report this company."

"Are you threatening me, Marcella?"

"No, just a friendly warning. I love my job and don't want to have to quit, but I will if I have to Alec."

Marcella turned back around and walked out the door, before he could reply. She walked fast, her heart racing and her hands shook. "Oh my God, what have I done," she whispered to herself.

Chapter Six

Diego Martinez, Drug Kingpin of the South; particularly the Georgia/Florida areas, sat at his cafe table next to the pool of his sprawling 15,200 Square foot Mediterranean home, drinking an espresso and puffing on a Montecristo 1935 cigar.

He lives in the elite Tuxedo Park area of Buckhead, only minutes from Atlanta. Tuxedo Park is a gated community where homes start in the millions and go back a century, with six bedrooms, twelve bathrooms, a separate wing that includes a House manager apartment, as well as a guest living area in the East wing, it's more of a compound than a house. As it is, Diego's home is worth $9.5 million in the current market.

All the homes boast beautiful landscaped gardens, lush greenery and long driveways. Privacy is a perk, and building neighbor friendships, non-existent, which is just the way he likes it. The fewer people that got in his business, the better.

Diego's cell phone was laying on the table when it started ringing. The number was a familiar one, but one he didn't usually get calls from.

"Alec my friend, this is a surprise. What can I do for you?"

"We have a problem."

"How can that be, I received word from my man that everything was finished and ready to go."

"He's not the problem, exactly."

"Then who is?"

"My assistant slash manager happened to leave the office late last night and inadvertently walked into the plant and saw your guy."

"And?"

"She has pictures of everything he was doing? She questioned me about it this morning."

"I see, and what did you tell her?"

"I told her I'd look into it and take care of it, but she said if I didn't, she would go to the authorities herself, with the pictures."

"I guess you know what you need to do then, am I right?"

"You want me to go to the cops?"

"That's what you think I meant? No, don't be stupid. I want you to take care of your problem, Alec and I want it done before the boats ship out. Do we understand each other amigo? It's that or you will pay the price, if this goes south."

"Isn't there another way? Can't I make up a story about me going to the authorities, and they have the guy in custody, then whenever your "associate is supposed to show up, from now on, I make sure she is out of the building way before he gets here, end of story and no one gets hurt?"

"Alec, Alec, Alec... it doesn't work that way. She knows too much. Now do it, or else. If you need ideas, ask, but make sure it is taken care of by the end of business, today.

You know she can have your butt thrown in jail, right? She has no idea about me or who my guy even is, she just has a picture of him. He looks like many other Latino men walking the streets of Atlanta."

"Marcella is an innocent bystander."

"ENOUGH! Maybe I need to have my boys come over to that palatial home of yours on the lake and have a little chat with you about loyalty."

"Fine! It'll be handled tonight. Those goons of yours are not to set one foot on my property."

"Make her disappear, and they won't. You took chemistry in high school right?"

"Of course, why?"

"It may come in handy, if you know what I mean."

And with those parting words, he hung on Alec, shaking his head.

"Miguel, go grab Juan and meet me in my office in ten minutes."

"We'll be right there Jefe."

Diego walked the perimeter of the courtyard that circled around the pool, and opened the sliding glass door that led to his office. He stood in front of the small wet bar that was behind his desk and looked into the mirror at himself. Diego was in his early fifties, close to 6 feet 2 inches, with a slim, but lean muscular build, short black hair and eyes as dark as pitch.

A knock at the door brought him out of his head. "Enter."

Two large gentlemen entered Diego's office, looking like they were ready to take on the world. Miguel, who is Diego's go to for encouraging buyers to pay up, as well as pseudo bodyguard, stood at attention wearing a black suit, black sunglasses and carrying a Glock 19 in his waistband, alongside Juan, who answers to Miguel, also wearing a black suit and sunglasses but is not as tall or bulky, but still exceptionally capable of some serious damage waited for the boss to begin.

"Gentlemen, sit. I have a job for you. I need you both to keep an eye on Mr. Brighton. He is supposed to be taking care of a problem by the end of the day, and I want to make sure he does as he's told."

Both men nodded, then Miguel piped up, "what exactly is he supposed to have done by the end of the day, Jefe?"

"His office manager has become a liability and Mr. Brighton needs to take care of her. Make sure he does."

"Yes Jefe."

"Go, keep an eye on him."

Both men exited the office, and Diego sat at his desk shaking his head. "The cartels in Juarez would never have this issue. I sometimes wish I was still there. Underlings listened and did what they were told, no questions asked and those who happened to be careless, disappeared," he said aloud, to himself.

Chapter Seven

Marcella was just packing up her office for the night, when Alec knocked on her door.

"Can I come in?"

"Of course, it's your company, I'm just an employee," she said.

"You're not just an employee, Mar. I hope you know that. Question...do you have time to go get a drink with me at Regent Cocktail Bar?"

"Um, I'm not sure that's a great idea. Did you contact the authorities about our earlier discussion yet?"

"That's kind of what I wanted to talk to you about. I don't want to do it here though. Too many eyes and ears, if you know what I mean."

Marcella had a gnawing feeling in the pit of her stomach that had been growing exponentially all day and now alarm bells were going off in her head.

But she wanted to hear what he had to say. "Okay, I can join you for one drink. I'll meet you there."

"Great, how about we say, in thirty minutes? I have a couple calls to make before I leave."

"I'll be there."

Alec was just about to leave her office when he turned around, "can you wait while I finish up, and then we'll head over there, together?" He smiled his enigmatic smile, hoping she'd agree.

After close to a thirty-second silence, she agreed to wait for him.

"I'll pop over once I'm ready."

Marcella sat back into her chair, palms covering her eyes, when she let a small sigh escape. She quickly ran through her mind, possible scenarios that may arise tonight, and not one of them was good. Reaching for her phone, she scrolled through her contacts to see if there was anyone she could trust to send the pictures too, in case something were to happen to her.

It wasn't looking good. "This is what I get for being a workaholic... no boyfriend, but I do have

Francesa. God bless Francesca. She would have zero clue why she was getting these pictures in an email from me, but she's all I have.

How could I have let this happen?" she questioned herself.

She was looking through all the pictures she took, zooming in, double checking that what she indeed saw were drugs being placed inside the steering column, before she sent the message to her friend.

"Damn it, how could this be happening?"

"What's that?"

Marcella shrieked, her phone went flying, and she nearly fell on the floor.

"Jesus Alec, don't do that!"

"Sorry, I just overheard you say, how could this be happening and I wondered what that meant. I didn't mean to startle you."

As she picked her phone up, checked to make sure the screen didn't shatter, Marcella looked at Alec, making sure to keep a nonplussed look on her face as she lied and said, "I was just reviewing some purchase orders, and they seem to be all wrong, but I'll check with the accounting department. Were you ready to go?"

"Yeah, I just packed everything and made the calls I needed, so we can leave now."

"Great," she lamented, as she hit send and grabbed her purse and briefcase.

They were in the parking lot when Alec directed her to his Land Rover that was parked close to the entrance of the building.

She hiked herself up into the plush leather seat, buckled her seat belt and said nothing as they headed toward Atlanta.

The drive to Regent felt oddly uncomfortable, so Marcella broke the awkward silence by asking, "have you been on the lake recently?"

Alec had eyes on the road, a death grip on the steering wheel, in his own little world when Marcella cleared her throat loud enough that he jerked his head in her direction and scowled at her. The look made her shrink back into her seat.

"I'm sorry Mar, did you say something," he asked, trying to recover himself.

"I was just wondering if you've been out on Lanier lately."

"Not in a couple of weeks. I am hoping to get out this weekend though, the weather is supposed to be beautiful. How about you?"

She noticed his demeanor go from pure hatred to sweet as honey within seconds, and went with it, for the moment. He could be under some stress, especially after what she brought to his attention earlier. Alec never spoke to her in such tones before, so she would give him the benefit of the doubt.

"Last time I was on my boat was last Thursday, after work. It wasn't windy and the temperature was perfect, so I took it out for maybe an hour, and I was back before dark. There had been quite a few boats out that evening, actually."

"I plan on taking mine out Saturday, for sure. All the boats that are supposed to go out this month, will be picked up Friday, so I'll give myself the weekend to relax."

"Good idea. You need to take a break now and then, or you'll go mad, am I right?"

"Absolutely."

The conversation seemed to be flowing easy enough now, but she really wanted to ask him if he called the authorities yet, but being that he nearly jumped down her throat a minute ago over an innocent question, she was still leary.

As she looked out the window, she noticed they were getting closer to downtown Atlanta, and Regent Cocktail Bar. Her thoughts were along the lines of, maybe one drink and then bring it up, when he's a little more relaxed.

The bar wasn't located directly in downtown Atlanta, but close to Buckhead, in the Buckhead Village District. The bar was located on the third floor of the American Cut Atlanta, which is a high end steak and seafood restaurant.

Alec parked his Land Rover on the street a block down from their destination. Marcella got out of the car and joined him on the sidewalk. They made their way down Peachtree Road and walked into American Cut Atlanta and headed for the elevator.

The Regent Cocktail Bar has indoor and outdoor seating. Since the sun was setting and the temperatures weren't stifling, Alec had the host seat them outside. Immediately the waitress descended on their table, taking drink orders.

Marcella ordered a Negroni, which is an Italian cocktail consisting of one part Campari, one part Gin, one part Sweet red Vermouth. It is considered an aperitif and stirred, not shaken, garnished with an orange peel and served over ice in an old fashion or rocks glass.

Alec ordered a Manhattan straight up. A Manhattan is a whiskey drink that uses Rye or Canadian Whiskey, along with Sweet red Vermouth, a dash of Angostura bitters and a Maraschino cherry as a garnish.

The bar was famous for making the drinks from the prohibition times and was notorious for having an upscale crowd.

Marcella noticed after the waitress left, that Alec's eyes were darting all around them, like he was looking for someone or something. It was making her nervous, so she focused on the southern skyline instead. The sun was setting over the city and it was beautiful with its pink and orange hues. It took her mind off of the bad feeling she was getting in the pit of stomach.

After their drinks arrived, the ominous silence continued, driving her crazy. Marcella took a large gulp of her Negroni, shivered at the amount of alcohol she just swallowed and gathered her nerve up to break the silence. She felt her insides instantly warm as the mixture of Campari, gin and vermouth went down.

"Now or never," she thought to herself. "Alec, we need to talk. Did you contact the authorities about the drugs?"

Alec gasped and sprayed a bit of his manhattan on the hand that held his drink. "Jeez Mar, don't say that out loud, you don't know who may be listening." He was clearly agitated with her and the way she blurted her statement out. He cleaned off his mouth and hand with one of the cocktail napkins, appeared to regain control and gaped at her. "This is not the place to talk about this," he hissed.

Marcella looked at him, indignant, "A simple yes or no Alec, it's not a hard question."

Diego's men Miguel and Juan, sat at the inside part of Regent Bar, keeping an eye on the couple sitting outside and watched the incident unfold.

Juan said in a low voice, "Jefe is not going to like this, they're causing a scene. Do you think we should call him?" He pulled his phone out to call Diego Martinez and report the incident, when Miguel took a hold of his hand. "What are you doing, shouldn't we let Jefe know," Juan asked.

Miguel continued his observance of the couple, but in a low voice said, "we will let him know. I'll text him that maybe he should give his boat runner a quick call."

Juan put his phone back into his coat pocket and let Miguel text their boss. He turned back around toward the bartender and asked for a Paloma, which is a Mexican cocktail made with tequila, fresca and lime. After Miguel sent his text, he shouted to the bartender, "make that two Paloma's." He nodded to him and began mixing their drinks.

*****   *****

Marcella finished her drink and flagged their waitress down for another since she wasn't getting a straight answer out of Alec, but she wouldn't give up until she did. The alcohol coursing through her was the bit of liquid courage she needed to keep questioning him.

"Alec, are you in trouble or something? Being blackmailed? What? Obviously you know that there are drugs going into the steering columns of the boats. You haven't denied it, so I have to assume you knew." She kept her voice low, so no one would over hear her.

Alec ran his hands through his short hair, clearly trying to think of what to say, when his phone started going off. He checked the screen and stood quickly, "I have to take this." He walked a good thirty feet away from her, so she couldn't hear.

"Why are you calling me, right now? You are to never call me on this number."

"Oh Mr. Brighton, I will call you whenever I see fit, and from what I gather, you're not at home."

"That's correct. I am out having a drink with a friend. What do you want?"

"Have you taken care of the little matter we discussed earlier?"

"Not yet, but I will."

"I know you haven't. Now, if you need me to take over, I will, but it'll cost you."

Alec began scanning the area, wondering how Diego knew that he had yet to pull off the job. "Are you following me?"

"No, not me, but I need to know that what I ask of you is being done. Just remember that, Mr. Brighton."

He went to reply, but the line went dead. "Damn it!"

Alec walked back to where Marcella was sipping on her new drink. "Everything okay," she asked.

"It's fine." He grabbed his drink and gulped the whole thing in one swallow and flagged down the waitress for another.

"Maybe you should slow down on the alcohol, Alec. I can call an Uber to pick me up, but you shouldn't drive.

*****   *****

Miguel received a text from Diego telling him he took care of it, but Alec needed a little extra encouragement.

*****   *****

The waitress set the drinks on the table and left the tab with Alec. Apparently she thought they both had enough for one evening.

Marcella was feeling the effects of her Negroni and figured she may have quite the headache tomorrow, but at the moment she was too tense to care, because the drinks seemed to take off the edge a bit. She held her third drink in her hand, sipping it slower than the last two. "Are you going to talk to me Alec? I want the truth, did you know about the drugs going out of our plant inside the boats?"

Alec debated on giving her the whole truth or just partial, not that it was going to matter after tonight, he thought. "Yes, I knew about it, who do you think authorized it?"

Marcella sat gobsmacked, "I don't know what to say." She took a long sip of her drink and sat there utterly speechless.

"There's nothing to say Mar, it's not your problem. It's my company," he stated, as he picked up his drink and took a swig.

"I beg your parddddoon..." she slurred. Marcella felt her tongue tingle and her limbs feel funny. Either the alcohol was kicking in, she thought, or... then she had a moment of panic. Was something in her drink? Her brain continued to get fuzzy by the second.

"Mar, you should really slow down on the drinks," Alec said, almost laughing. He chugged the rest of his drink and slammed the glass on the table. He looked at Marcella, and she was three sheets to the wind. "I think we should go now."

Alec bent over to grab Marcella's shoulder to get her attention, "Let's go Mar." He noticed she could barely open her eyes. "Crap!"

He grabbed hold of her around the waist and brought her to a standing position. With one arm around her waist and another holding her arm, he walked with her to the elevator. Once inside, he hit the button for the first floor and held on to her. "C'mon Mar, wake up. I can't carry you out of here."

The elevator doors swished open, Alec had a hold of Marcella, and he made his way for the exit when his arms felt weak and his head started swimming. His vision was blurry, but he noticed something in front of him and heard voices asking questions, but couldn't understand what they said. "What," he asked.

Everything then went dark and silent.

Chapter Eight

The waves on Lake Lanier reached three feet, with mild white caps. A storm was brewing and even with a forty-foot cabin cruiser, the combination of the wind and the waves rocked the boat back and forth.

Alec lay on the back deck of his forty foot Chris-Craft cabin cruiser, passed out. His eyes struggled to open, as nausea and a raging headache came to the forefront of his mind. He opened his eyes, looking back and forth, disoriented and having no clue where he was. The boat lurched to the one side from the wind that seemed to be picking up more. Alec rolled to his side trying to gain some balance and tried pushing the nausea aside, so he could stand up and get his bearings.

"How the hell did I get on my boat," he whispered to himself. Grabbing a hold of the railing, he pulled himself to a semi standing position to look over the side of the boat. All around him was water, the shore was nowhere to be seen.

Fear and anxiety seeped into his brain. "What did I do? How did I get so far out here?" These are just a few of the questions plaguing Alec's mind.

The anchor had been dropped and kept him where he was, thankfully, but where he was, was still a mystery and how he got there, riddled his brain with more questions than he answers for.

He made his way inside the cabin, looking for a bottle of water and some much-needed aspirin. Alec noticed the purse, immediately. He knew who it belonged to, as well. His anxiety and panic ratcheted up ten-fold. He moved throughout the cabin, checking the bedroom, bathroom and kitchen, but found no one.

Alec moved to the back deck where he woke up, looked around and saw something glinting in what sunlight there was. It lay in the corner. He bent to see what it was, picked it up and held it between his thumb and forefinger. "Oh sweet Jesus, Marcella." He held her diamond stud earring in his fingers, staring at it, like it was a crystal ball that would show him what he wanted to know. Taking his eyes off the earring, he looked overboard to see if anything was floating in the area. Squatting down, with his head in his hands, Alec tried to recall the events from the night before, but nothing was coming to him, except him being with Marcella at the bar.

He took note of a tiny spot of blood on the deck. Alec stood and bent over the railing to throw up. "My God, what did I do?"

A phone started ringing inside the cabin area, so after wiping his mouth with his arm, he stumbled into the cabin to look for the source of the noise. He found the phone on the floor, picked it up, not even looking to see who it was and answered it, "Hello," he said tersely.

The person on the other end was quiet for a moment before responding. "I must have the wrong number," said a female. "I was looking for Marcella Gallo."

Alec immediately threw the phone out of his hand, like it was a burning rod, scorching his skin. "Son of a..."

Not even five seconds later, the phone on the floor began to ring again. Alec reached for the phone, declined the call and shut it down completely. If someone was looking for Marcella, all they would have to do is track her phone through the towers. He didn't even know where she was, and her purse and belongings were here with him. Alec was feeling sicker by the minute. He needed to get back to shore, contact Diego and take a drive over to Marcella's house to see if she's there.

His strength was waning, as he pulled the anchor back into the boat. This was one hell of a hangover, he thought as he started the engines up and maneuvered his boat through the high waves to get back to his dock. He hadn't yet figured out how far out on the Lake he actually was, but looking at the maps, he was guessing he was a good 20 miles out. Lake Lanier was one of the biggest man-made lakes in the country. It runs 44 miles and has 692 miles of shoreline.

Alec started seeing the shoreline and figured he was on the Gainesville, Georgia end, which meant he had to make his way farther South to where his house sat, which is closer to Buford. His heart pounded in his chest and with each thud, his panic rose. Questions rolled around in his head, "Did I kill her and dump her body in the lake? Did she jump overboard to get away from me?"

Slamming his hand on the wheel, "why can't I remember? Diego is going to kill me, if she's still alive, anyway. That's what I was supposed to do last night, maybe I blocked the memories on purpose, so

I wouldn't remember killing her. Is that even possible?" He stood there and let the thoughts form. "If I had taken a couple hits of the product last night, that may explain things, but that had to have been some good stuff. I'd never had that type of high before, where I lost memories. It usually makes me euphoric and relaxed."

After an hour of driving, Alec could see his dock in the distance, and he breathed out a small sigh.

Chapter Nine

Francesca Rose, pulled to a screeching halt in Marcella's driveway and ran to the door pounding and ringing the doorbell. She didn't see Marcella's car and couldn't hear anything through the door, either.

Francesca, a 32-year-old stylist that works at the exclusive shop Jovani, in Atlanta and one of Marcella's only friends, started to panic. Francesca's jet black hair was pulled back into a high ponytail, showing off her high cheekbones, azure blue eyes and naturally tanned skin, but with the wind picking up, her hair was blowing all around her. She wore camel colored pants with a black blouse and four inch Prada heels that accentuated her long frame. She knew this wasn't like her friend to not answer her phone, much less let anyone else pick it up. That's what tipped her off, the man answering her cell phone was completely out of character and something was certainly wrong.

Francesca dialed the office number that she had for Marcella and the receptionist picked up, "Good Morning Atlantic Sea, how can I help you?"

"I'd like to speak to Marcella Gallo, please."

"I'm sorry, I'm not sure where Miss Gallo is. Her car is here, but I haven't seen her. Can I take a message?"

"Her car is there, but you haven't seen her?"

"Yes, ma'am."

"Can you do me a favor? Can you look in her office real quick and see if her purse or briefcase is in there?"

"Sure, I can go check. Is everything alright?"

Francesca wasn't sure how to answer that question, so she answered her truthfully, "I'm not sure."

"I see. Hold on while I go check her office."

It felt like an eternity waiting for the receptionist to get back on the line. Her patience was starting to waver and her blood pressure creeped up every ten seconds she waited. Finally, the phone clicked and the girl spoke hesitantly. "Ma'am, her purse and briefcase are not in her office anywhere. I asked a couple of people around the office, and they have not seen her since yesterday. Should I call the police?"

Francesca shut her eyes, pulling the fear back "No, I'll call them, thank you. If you happen to hear from her, can you please call me as soon as you can?" She rattled off her cell phone number to the young lady and hung up.

"Where are you, Marcella?"

She went around back to check out the sliding patio door that led to the dock. Francesca peaked through the window and didn't notice anything out of order, so she called the local police department to see what she could do.

"When was the last time anyone saw Miss Gallo?" The officer was taking notes before sending someone out.

She had to think... "The receptionist at her office said no one had seen her since yesterday. She's never missed a day of work, she's never late and when I called her cell phone earlier, I thought I had the wrong number when a man answered and after I said who I was looking for, the phone line went dead. I tried her number again, it rang a few times and went to voicemail. Now when I call it, it goes straight to voicemail like it's been shut off."

"Okay, normally we have to wait 24 hours before a missing persons report is taken, but in this case I am going to send someone over to her address. Are you still at her residence?"

"Yes, I'm still here. I'll wait for the officer."

"Perfect, someone should be there shortly."

"Thank you."

Francesca went back to her car, and waited until she saw a patrol car approach fifteen minutes later. She stepped out of her vehicle as the officer started walking toward her. He was tall, built like a linebacker, good-looking and young. She thought he was maybe in his early twenties. "Great, they sent me the rookie."

"Are you Ms. Rose," the officer asked.

"Yes, I am, and please call me Francesca. I'm the one who called about Marcella Gallo going missing."

"Okay Francesca, I'm Officer Wade Montgomery," he said, holding out his hand to shake hers. "Let me just take a quick look around the perimeter of the property and I will be back with you. Can you stay for a little while to answer some questions?"

"Absolutely, I'll call into work and tell them I'll be late."

While she made the call to the shop, Officer Montgomery walked toward the back of the property, where he found a small speed boat at the dock. He walked out to where the boat sat in the water, and did a cursory look at the inside. At first glance, nothing seemed to be out of place and it didn't appear to have any noticeable marks or anything on it, so he continued back up to the rear of the house where the patio sat. He checked the sliding glass door to see if it had been tampered with, but it showed no signs of a break in. After looking into the house from the patio door, he couldn't see any signs of a struggle, and nothing seemed to be knocked over. From what he was seeing so far, nothing was amiss. He continued his walk around the other side of the property, still not seeing anything wrong. He met back up with Francesca at her car.

"Did you notice anything? I looked around before I called and didn't notice anything, myself, but you know more of what to look for, than I do."

"Everything here seems to be fine. When was the last time you spoke to Miss Gallo? Did she say anything about going out of town?"

"I talked to her briefly a day and a half ago, I guess, but she never mentioned anything about leaving town. She would have told me if she was leaving."

"Did she sound okay when you spoke to her last? Maybe she was whisked away on a romantic weekend as a surprise."

"No, that's not it, I know it. She doesn't have a boyfriend and as far as dating, she was much too busy at work for that. She works at Atlantic Sea, Inc. She's the Assistant to the CEO and the Office Manager; her work is her life. I know something isn't right. When I called her office, the receptionist said that her car is there, but she isn't. I even had her check Marcella's office to see if her purse and briefcase were in it, but they weren't.

"I'm going to head over to Atlantic Sea, Inc., and speak to her boss. Hopefully he'll have an idea of where she is. You can head to work now and if you'll give me a number where you can be reached, if I find out anything, I'll call you."

Francesca's stomach plummeted and she felt sick. Something was wrong and that worried her. She took a business card out of her purse and handed it over to Officer Montgomery.

"Please call me as soon as you know something, anything. I don't care what time it is."

"Of course ma'am, I'll see that you are informed."

"I appreciate it, thank you."

They both headed back to their cars and went their separate ways.

Chapter Ten

Alec pulled into the parking lot of Atlantic Sea, Inc., like he did so many times before, except today, he didn't feel the same excitement as he usually did. For one, he still had a raging headache, even after downing three aspirin and took a quick hit of the stuff and second, he still had no recollection of how he got on his boat.

He pulled his Land Rover into his normal spot, grabbed his coffee from the cup holder and stepped out, only to see Marcella's silver BMW parked where it usually is, two spots down from him.

"Great, she must be here," he said under his breath.

Alec made his way through the double doors where he saw one of the security guys talking to a police officer. "Fabulous, now what," he thought to himself.

The security guard flagged him over to where he and the officer were talking.

"Sir, Officer Montgomery is inquiring about the whereabouts of Ms. Gallo. It seems she may be missing."

The room started to spin on its axis, and he thought he was going to vomit right there on the officer. "Um... what do you mean missing? I saw her car in the parking lot."

"It is sir, but after looking through the security tapes from the parking lot, her car never moved after she arrived yesterday morning." the guard said.

"But, we did see the two of you leaving around 6pm last night, together in your car, Mr. Brighton," Officer Montgomery added. "Can you tell me where you two went and where Ms. Gallo might be right now?"

Alec felt the color drain from his face, he had no idea where she could be. She was definitely on his boat at some point, he knew that. He still carried the diamond earring in his pocket that he found on the deck, and her purse, he put it in his safe that is in his closet, but as to where she is now, he just didn't know.

"We went to The Regent Cocktail bar for a drink after work to talk about some business items, but that was the last I saw of her." Of that, he was sure of it, but after they went to leave, he still couldn't remember.

"Did anyone see you both at The Regent," the officer asked.

"I… I don't know. We sat outside at the Rooftop bar, our waitress was a female, with red hair, maybe in her late 20s. The place was packed as it usually is, so lots of people had to have seen us."

"Okay, that gives me something to check out. Did you and Ms. Gallo have a romantic relationship, at all?"

"No, of course not. She was my assistant and office manager. We were on friendly terms, as she has worked here for over five years." He tried to sound contrite, but his stomach was churning with acid.

"I'll be heading to Regent then, and I will be in touch with you, Mr. Brighton."

"Oh, okay. You obviously know where to find me. By the way, how did you know where to find me and that Marcella worked here?" He was curious as to who reported her missing.

Montgomery looked back at Alec, his brows drawn together, he didn't entirely trust him. "A friend of hers," and he left it at that and walked out.

Alec took off for his office, needing to make a call.

"Mr. Brighton, do you have a minute?" His secretary was holding up an envelope when he snaked past her, not even acknowledging her presence.

Sitting at his desk, he turned his computer on, going rigid when he saw a small manila envelope sitting on his desk, sealed and clasped shut, with his name scrolled on it. He stared at it for a beat before picking it up and opening it. Looking inside, he didn't see it at first, then tipped the envelope over so the object inside could slide out. In his palm sat a diamond stud with blood spatter on it. He dropped it and ran for the bathroom that was attached to his office and vomited.

Alec rinsed his mouth out, splashed cold water on his face and looked at himself in the mirror. "What happened last night?" Gathering a towel to dry his face and hands, they shook nervously, and he knew he needed to get himself under control or everything would fall apart.

Walking back to his desk, he bent down to retrieve the earring from the floor along with the envelope and placed the earring back inside, sealed it up and took it to the safe he had in his office that is hidden behind a large picture that had the first boat he manufactured on it, so to open it, it requires his fingerprint and retina scan. After going through the security process, he opened the safe where he kept a small stash of cash, a black box, as well as a small baggie of the heroine Diego gave him to try. He kept one at work and one at home, in case he felt the need. Holding the baggie, he thought about taking another hit, but put it back, since he'd already had one at home, more than that, and he might not be able to function. He pulled the black box out, opened it and inside was a 9 mm Glock. Alec placed the small envelope inside with the gun and closed it back up.

Sitting back at his desk, Alec pulled up his email, scanning all the new ones that he'd received over the last twelve or so hours. He saw one that looked off, so he clicked on it, not recognizing the sender, but as he started reading it, his heart started thudding in his chest.

Since you were unable to take care of business, it has been taken care of for you. You're welcome.

"Jesus, what does that mean?" It took him two beats for everything to click into place. "She's dead."

Chapter Eleven

Officer Wade Montgomery sat at his desk, staring at his computer, working on reports when his phone rang. "Officer Montgomery," he said a little too brusquely.

"Officer Montgomery, this is Francesca Rose. We spoke a couple of days ago, when I reported my friend Marcella Gallo missing."

Wade put the palm of his hand to his twitching eye in mild frustration. "Yes, I remember. I am still looking for leads on this case. I went to the Regent Cocktail bar, which was where Marcella and her boss Alec Brighton had gone that evening, however, I'm still waiting on the waitress that waited on them to call. She wasn't working the day I was there."

"I see. You have other leads besides that one that you're looking into?"

"Not at this time. I'm sorry."

There was a large amount of activity forming at the front of the bull pen where the detectives sat. They were gathered around a TV and talking louder than normal. Wade wanted to see what all the hubbub was.

"Ms. Rose, I will call you as soon as I know something, I promise."

"Okay, thank you...."

He didn't even wait for her to hang up before he slammed the phone on the cradle and ran toward the commotion.

"Hey, what's going on? Why all the commotion?"

Police Chief Holt Montgomery and Wade's father looked at him, "Engineers that were dredging Lake Lanier came across a body, pretty far down. Only thing left was a skeleton. So, I'm guessing it's been down there a long time, if all that's left is bones."

"Oh, I thought it might have been something else."

"Sorry to disappoint you son. Have you gotten any new information on the missing persons case you're working on?"

"I'm still waiting on the waitress from Regent to get back to me. She was more than likely the last one to see Ms. Gallo. Where are they taking the skeleton that was found?"

"The Medical Examiner will do her thing and determine how old it is and may find out what happened to it."

"Okay. Well, I am taking off, that girl has to be back to work by now, so I'm heading down to the Regent Cocktail bar, if you need me."

"Keep me updated, Wade."

*****   *****

Wade parked his patrol car in front of the Regent Cocktail bar, grabbed his notebook and pen and made his way to the third floor bar area.

He approached the bartender, "I'm looking for one of your waitresses, she has red hair, mid to late twenties."

"You're looking for Haven. She should be here at 5, for her shift. If you want to take a seat, I'll let her know you're here and want to talk to her, as soon as she gets in."

"That would be great, thank you." Leaning over the bar, Wade asked," can I get a Coke while I wait?"

"Sure, coming right up. You don't want a beer or anything, or are you still on duty?"

"No thanks, I'm still on duty. I'm here in an official capacity."

"Haven's not in trouble is she," the bartender asked, nervously.

"No, I just need to ask her a few questions about a couple she waited on a few days ago, the woman is missing."

"Seriously? Who is it? I may have seen them."

Wade brought up a picture on his phone of Marcella that Francesca had given him, and he turned his phone around so the bartender could take a look at it. "Do you remember her, by chance?"

The guy at the bar took the phone and looked at the attractive lady in the picture, he did remember her, she looked much happier in this photo than she had the other night. "I was here, but I didn't have any contact with them. I do remember seeing them though. She didn't look too happy when they were outside drinking. The guy she was with, I've seen here multiple times. He's a real jerk when he drinks, too. He's a bigwig boat dealer or something."

"Did it look like they were fighting at all, or just talking?"

The bartender passed him his drink, as he took a moment to remember the couple as they sat outside a few nights ago.

"No, they were definitely not just talking friendly, and they weren't arguing technically, but it looked more like she was irritated with him though, for sure. Haven may have a better take on their situation since she was with them multiple times that night, serving their drinks."

"So they were drinking pretty heavily?"

"Oh yeah, and one right after the other, too. I was wondering how they were going to get home. They must have left when I was back in the storeroom getting more bottles, because I didn't see them leave."

'Thanks for all your help. I'll wait until Haven gets here and ask her a few more questions, if you don't mind."

"No man, that's fine, take your time."

Wade took in the surroundings of the swanky bar and felt a little out of place, especially in uniform. This place was upper-crust, not blue collar. Give him a small bar that had pool tables and dart boards lining the back wall any day.

He looked toward the elevator as it opened when a young red head emerged. This must be Haven, he thought. She was young, with red hair and tattoos lining her left arm, but she was dressed for the atmosphere here, with her black dress pants, white button down shirt, red silk necktie, black shoes and her makeup was neat and well done, as were her nails. Professionally done, Wade thought. She was attractive, he noticed.

"Excuse me, Haven?"

She looked at him, eyes wide, her lips parted slightly, and confusion set in. "Yes, who wants to know?"

He stood up with his hand out to her, "Officer Wade Montgomery, I need to ask you a few questions about a couple you waited on a few days ago, can we sit and talk for a few minutes? I've already cleared it with your boss over there."

"Ss..sure," she stuttered.

He saw the scared look on her face and wanted to ease her tension, "I promise, this will be painless. I just have a couple questions."

"Okay, how can I help you?"

Wade pulled the picture of Marcella up again on his phone and showed it to her, "do you remember this lady here the other night? She was with a gentleman, Alec Brighton, the CEO of Atlantic Sea, Inc. I can pull up his picture too, if it will help?"

Haven stared at the woman in the picture. Yeah, she remembered her and the jerk she was with. They were drinking like fish and looked angry,

"Yes, they were here the other night. I waited on them for a couple of hours. They didn't sip their drinks, they gulped them. And they asked for one right after the other."

"Would you say they were on date or did it look more platonic?"

"Definitely not on a date. They seemed to be colleagues, or maybe frenemies would be a more accurate description. He was mean mugging her practically the whole night. Of course, she was giving some serious death stares at him, too. Why are you asking?"

Wade was jotting all this down in his notebook. "The young lady is missing, and I am trying to find out what happened to her. This seems like the last place she was seen. Did you ever overhear their conversations at all?"

"She's missing? Wow, that's horrible. Every time I came back to clear glasses or take down a new drink order from them, they seemed to quiet any kind of conversation they were having. I'm sorry I can't be of more help."

"No problem, you gave me more than you think. I appreciate it. If you can think of anything else, here's my card. My office number and cell number are both on there," he said, handing her the business card he took from his pocket.

Haven smiled back and graciously accepted the card and stowed it away in her purse. "Well, I really have to get started on my shift."

"Of course, and I need to pay my tab." He held up his empty glass.

"Nah, I got this," she said as she turned away from him and walked to the bar.

Wade gave her and the bartender a wave of thanks as he headed out.

Chapter Twelve
Medical Examiner's Office

Medical Examiner Joyce Brooks had the skeletal remains of the body that had been fished out of Lake Lanier on her table. Dr. Brooks, a 54-year-old Mom of two boys thought she had seen everything, but you just never know what crazy case will come up within your career, she thought.

Even looking at the remains in front of her, without doing any tests so far, she thought the remains could be twenty plus years old, but she also knew that you can never judge a body by its skeleton. She hoped she'd never lose that sense of humor. Laughing to herself, she started to do a cursory look over the remains. Being that she also has a degree in forensic anthropology, Dr. Brooks immediately determined that the remains were definitely those of a female, just by the pelvic bone structure.

With her hand-held tape recorder in hand, she began to document her initial findings. "Jane Doe, found in the water of Lake Lanier, September 26, 2021, at 17:08 by city engineers. Upon initial glances, the skeletal remains look to be in good condition, some joint tissue has been eaten away from the bones, so length of time in the water is still unknown, but looking at the pelvic bone area, I am concluding that the remains are that of a female. However, age, race, height and cause of death still need to be determined. I will be performing a multitude of tests shortly, but first I will separate the bones. More to follow as tests are being done."

Dr. Brooks grabbed her tape measure to get the length of the skull, femur and tibia, as well as the ankle and foot, so she can start estimating the height of her Jane Doe. There are a couple of ways to determine the height of her remains and the one she is using is called the anatomical method. Once she measures the bones, she will also take into account the soft tissue at the joints, scalp and soles of the feet. This will add height. It's not an exact science, but it gives her an estimate within an inch.

She picked up her tape recorder from the table and hit the record button again, after she made her calculations. "After measuring each leg bone, skull, spinal cord, and adding in for the ankle, foot and soft tissue and joint areas, the estimated height of Jane Doe is 5'7, next I will try to determine the race of Jane, as well as age. I will start with measuring the cranial and facial areas of the skull, which will determine the race, then looking at the degree of fusion in the first and second sacral bodies and the medial clavicle epiphysis, that's the measuring of the long bone epiphysis (the round portions at the end of the bone) and the last. Doing this will help in determining the post-pubertal period or age of the victim). I will then compare my findings with those obtained from cadavers of all known ages, on record. Once complete, I will record those findings."

Dr. Brooks set to work and measured with precise calculations, the facial and cranial areas, and medial clavicle epiphysis, learning rather quickly that Jane was Caucasian and after comparing her findings of the clavicular epiphysis to those in the database, determined the remains were around 29-32 years of age at time of death.

While she put the skull on a lighted table, she pulled her SEM (Scanning Electron Microscope) over to get a better look at the teeth. Pulling the jaw bone apart slightly, she positioned the microscope over it and saw what looked like some kind of debris in between the two top front teeth. "Well well, what do we have here," she said as she grabbed a pair of tweezers.

She laid what was caught between the tweezers onto a glass plate and looked at it through the microscope, figuring it was probably a piece of algae or something from the lake. "Oh, definitely not algae. Looks like a piece of skin. Interesting... Did you bite someone before you ended up in the lake, Jane?"

Walking the glass dish into the lab that's adjacent to her morgue, she dropped the sample off to the lab technician, "I am going to need a DNA profile done on this as soon as you can, please."

The lab tech looked up from what he was doing, clearly annoyed by her interruption and shook his head in acknowledgment. "It may be a couple of days, I hope that's okay?"

"If that's the fastest you can do, then I guess I don't have a choice. This piece was pulled from the skeletal remains they found at the bottom of Lake Lanier, it was in between her teeth, so I am guessing she took a bite of someone before her death."

"If they were already skeletal remains, it probably happened years ago, what are they going to do?"

Dr. Brooks leveled a look at the technician, "I don't care how long it's been at the bottom of the lake, this woman is dead and her family is probably wondering whatever happened to her, and we are going to find out." She turned on her heel, walked out the door, slamming it shut behind her. "Damn Millennial."

She laid the bones out to look like a whole skeleton again, and took her SEM microscope to look more closely at the bone itself. She noticed the bone was rather clean for being in the lake, and it hadn't shown any signs of degradation yet, which surprised her. Grabbing her bone saw, Dr. Brooks cut the femur in half to examine the inside closer.

"Oh boy," she said, to herself. She went in search of her cell phone and placed a call to the Police department's chief Holt Montgomery.

"Chief Montgomery."

"Hey Holt, it's Joyce Brooks. You know the skeletal remains that were fished out of Lake Lanier earlier?"

"Yeah Joyce, I saw the news coverage. What's up?"

"Well, I thought the remains would probably be twenty plus years old... they're not. That body was only in the lake 1-3 days max."

"Really. Any idea on the cause of death yet or whether it's male or female?"

"It is a female, between the ages of 29-32, more than likely a Caucasian, cause of death is still to be determined."

"Okay, that's a start. I'm sending Wade over there to talk to you. He has a missing persons case that is fairly recent. I want him to talk to you, is that okay?"

"Sure, I'll be here for a while."

"Thanks Joyce, we'll be in touch. If you learn anything else, call me."

"One more thing, she had a piece of skin in between her two front teeth, I'm having the lab do a DNA analysis as we speak."

Chief Montgomery was quiet for a few seconds, absorbing the new information. "So, we're looking at a homicide, is that what you're trying to tell me?."

"Looks that way, yes."

"Wade will be down there shortly." He disconnected the line, and immediately called his son.

"Officer Montgomery," Wade said.

"Wade, I need you to get down to the M.E. 's office as soon as you can. There is a distinct possibility that the body found in the lake is that of your missing woman."

"What? How? It was a skeleton they found."

"Yeah well, Dr. Brooks called and said that the bones showed that it had only been in the lake maybe 1-3 days and it is a female, between the ages of 29-32, plus she's running a DNA analysis on a piece of skin found in between the teeth of the remains, so it's looking like a homicide. Get over there as soon as you can."

"I'm on my way. Thanks. Bye Dad."

*****   *****

Wade drove to the M.E's office on auto-pilot. He had a bad feeling in the pit of his stomach that the skeletal remains were that of his missing person case.

Once he parked and signed in, he made his way down the long hall to the last door on the right, where he knew there would be metal drawers on top of metal drawers, housing the dead remains of human beings. They will never again see their loved ones, never see the sun rise or set... "Jeez Montgomery, snap out of it!"

"Snap out of what," Dr. Brooks asked, as she stood in the doorway of the morgue.

Wade flinched. He didn't hear her come out. "Oh nothing, I was just talking to myself. You must be Dr. Brooks."

"And you must be Officer Wade Montgomery," she said, holding out her hand.

"Yes ma'am."

"Well, come on in. I'll show you everything I have so far and give you a copy of my notes thus far, as well. Does that sound like a plan?"

"Anything you can share with me will be great, thank you."

"Okay, come with me then. There are a couple of things I hadn't been able to tell Chief Montgomery, when I had him on the phone."

"He gave me most of the information you had already relayed to him, what was it that you didn't tell him?" The hair on the back of Wade's neck stood on end, anticipating what she forgot to mention to his dad.

"I did a couple of tests earlier on the surface area of the bone, as well as swabbing the inside to test for anything out of the ordinary. You know, being that the remains appear to only have been dead for a few days, it's not normal for it to be bone only. The results of the tests hadn't finished when I talked to the Chief, and I just got the results. This person was put into a bath or vat of lye. It dissolves the skin all the way to the bone and if she hadn't been dumped into the lake when she had, it would have dissolved the bones as well."

Wade thought he was going to vomit at the mental image the doctor's words were conjuring.

"Are you okay Officer Montgomery? You look a little green around the gills."

He looked her in the eye, took a deep breath, "yeah, I'm fine. Who would do such a thing to another human being?"

Dr. Brooks looked at him thoughtfully, "I ask myself that question every time I get a new body in here."

"Do you have any idea when you will have an ID on her, or if you can ID her?"

"I've extracted DNA from the bones and hopefully I'll have an answer for you. Do you know whether your missing person had any healed fractures or even if you can find out the name of the dentist she went to, I can request her dental records and do a comparison. The sooner we get her identified the better."

"I'll contact her friend that reported her missing and see if she can give me any information. Do you mind, I'm just going to make that call now?"

"Sure, by all means, do what you have to do."

Wade walked out into the hall for a little privacy; there, he pulled out his notebook to look for Marcella Gallo's friend, Francesca's cell phone number. He dialed and started pacing the hallway while it began to ring. She answered on the third ring, hesitation in her voice.

"Hello, this is Francesca."

"Ms. Rose, this is Officer Montgomery. I have a couple of questions for you, if you have a minute."

"Oh, sure, what do you need to know? Has there been any new information on Marcella?"

He could hear the anxiety in her voice, even over the phone. This was the part of his job he did not like.

"I was wondering if you could tell me if Marcella had ever had any broken bones, that you were aware of?"

"I've known her practically my whole life and as far as I know, she's never had any fractures, why?"

"Okay, would you happen to know the dentist she saw regularly? I'm trying to rule out some new information that has come to my attention. I can't really say for sure yet, until I know for sure, I'm sorry."

There was silence on the other end and Wade thought maybe she hung up or the call got disconnected.

"Francesca?"

"Yes, I'm here. Um, she saw the same dentist I did. We've gone to him since college, it's Dr. James Shorey."

She proceeded to give him the phone number for the dentist and resisted asking too many questions after that. Francesca wasn't ready to hear the answers.

"I appreciate your help. As soon as I know anything, I'll contact you. Marcella doesn't have any family in the area does she?"

"No, she's an only child and her parents had passed away almost six years ago in a car accident. Of course, her grandparents had passed away many years ago. My family and I are all she has." She cleared the lump forming in her throat before she continued. "Please let me know what you find out."

"I'll be in touch as soon as I know something. Thank you again for your help."

Running a hand down his face, Wade looked at the phone number Francesca provided for the dentist and called it, wanting to get this over with.

He got the dentist's secretary and after explaining the situation, she promised to gather the information he requested and said she would email everything over to the M.E. as soon as she got it all together.

There wasn't much more he could do here. Until they had the information from the dentist and the DNA back from the skin that was found in her teeth, they were just playing the waiting game.

Wade said his goodbyes to the doctor after she promised she would be in contact with him as soon as she had answers for him.

Chapter Thirteen

Chief Holt Montgomery was in his patrol car when his phone went off. Turning down the music he was listening to, he hit his Bluetooth connection to answer, "Chief Montgomery."

"Hi Holt, it's Joyce Brooks. I've got some interesting news for you."

Chief Montgomery looked heavenward, pretty sure the interesting news was not going to be good news. "Let's hear it."

"I got the dental records from that missing persons case Wade is working, and I have a perfect match to my Jane Doe. I will call Wade and let him know. But, that's not the only DNA test that came back. The sliver of skin I pulled from her teeth came back. It doesn't belong to anyone in CODIS, but it is the same DNA associated with another homicide that is in the system. It's a case that is still unsolved, obviously."

"Dang it, I'm going to have to bring in the FBI for this, aren't I?" He said it as more of a statement than a question to her, but she agreed anyway.

"Yes, it looks that way. Whoever killed this poor girl, has killed prior and has yet to be caught. Did Wade tell you the cause of death?"

"He did. That's just sick. Dissolving a body and dumping it into a lake is cold-blooded."

"Agreed. Well, let me call your son and give him the news. I just wanted to give you a heads up."

"Thanks Joyce, I appreciate it. I'm going to have to get a hold of my contact in the FBI. I believe he is working out of the Midwest office now, but he's good, so I am hoping he'll be able to come down here and help us with this."

"Good luck, let me know if you need anything from me. I'll have everything ready for them."

"Will do. Thanks."

*****   *****

Dr. Brooks put in a call to Officer Wade Montgomery as soon as she hung up with his father. She hated to tell him that his missing person was indeed deceased, but he knew it was going to be a possibility.

Wade picked up his cell on the second ring, noting the number that was calling. "Dr. Brooks, what have you got for me?"

"Wow, no hello," she said, slightly amused.

"Sorry, that was unprofessional of me. Hello Dr. Brooks, have you found anything out yet?"

"Officer Montgomery, I was just giving you a hard time. I do have some news for you. I'm sorry, but the remains are those of Marcella Gallo. Not only did the dental records confirm, but the DNA from the bone did as well."

Wade was silent for a breath before he responded. "I see. Was there anything else you were able to get?"

"Yes, actually there is. I have already talked to Chief Montgomery about this, but the DNA from the sliver of skin she had stuck between her teeth isn't showing up in CODIS, but it is showing up in another homicide that is still open. So whoever did this to Ms. Gallo is involved in another case and has so far successfully eluded the authorities, since there is no record in the system of who the DNA belongs to, he or she is still in the wind. And they have been for nearly twenty plus years."

"Great, so I guess the FBI will be called in now and I will be off the case."

"The FBI will be called in, but I'm not sure you'll be completely off the case. Will you please notify her next of kin though?"

"Of course. Her biological family is pretty much non-existent, but her best friend, the lady who reported her missing, is the closest thing she had to family from what I gathered. I will head over to her now. Thank you for all your help, Dr. Brooks."

"You're welcome. I'm just sorry it wasn't better news."

"Me too."

*****   *****

Officer Montgomery got the address of Francesca from the license database, he headed over to break the news to her. Again he thought, "this is the worst part of the job."

When Wade pulled into the driveway of the townhouse where Francesca lived, he saw the front door open before he made it out of his car. Her arms were wrapped around herself and the look of dread showed on her face. She knew why he was here.

"Miss Rose, can we go inside and talk?"

She looked him in the eyes, her own eyes welling up with tears, all she could manage was a shake of her head as she turned to go back inside the house.

Francesca stood in the main hallway, turning to face Wade, her fingers gripping her hair, "she's dead, isn't she?" Tears streamed down her delicate face. He took her hand in his, trying to take some of her pain from her, he whispered, "yes, I'm sorry she is."

She let him continue to hold her hand, because if she let go, she might drop to the ground. He was an anchor for her. "How," she choked out on a sob."

Wade gently kept her hand in his and guided her farther into the house to where he could set her down in a chair, then he would explain as much as could to her.

"I'm so sorry for your loss. We are going to do everything we can to catch whoever did this to your friend. We are actually bringing the FBI in on this."

Francesca looked at the officer, wide-eyed, "the FBI? Why?"

"I can't give you any specifics yet, but as soon as I can, I will."

"Is she the one they found in Lake Lanier, they said it was skeletal remains they found. How is that possible? It's only been a few days since she went missing."

Nodding in acknowledgment, Wade did not want to go into the details of how her friend died. "You really don't need to know how, trust me on this."

She barely heard him over her sobs.

Telling people that a loved one has died is emotionally draining, but to tell them that they have been murdered is a hundred times worse.

"Before I go, can I get you anything, or call someone to come over?"

With a weak smile, Francesca declined his offer and stood to walk him to the door. She touched his elbow faintly, "thank you for coming here in person. If you could keep me in the loop on everything, I would appreciate it."

"I will. And again, I am so sorry."

Chapter Fourteen

Jake Long, a special agent with the FBI's Midwest division, pulled on his neck tie, trying to loosen it. Jake wasn't one who enjoyed dressing up, but duty called. Not that he didn't look the part, but with his black wavy hair that he wore cropped close and his four day old beard growth on his olive colored skin, and his lean build, he could still pass for someone in his 30s, especially since he's held onto his college football days body, just sat at his desk, typing up his reports from the case he just finished, when his cell phone rang.

"FBI Special Agent Long."

"Jake, this is Chief Holt Montgomery, how are you?"

"Hey Chief, I'm good. Is this a friendly call or a professional call?" Jake already had a sneaking suspicion that it was professional, but he asked anyway.

"Unfortunately professional, this time. We caught a missing person's case a few days ago, and she was found at the bottom of Lake Lanier, or more accurately, her skeletal remains were found. Her skin was completely dissolved, leaving almost a pristine skeleton."

"Okay. I'm sorry to hear that, but why call me? This doesn't sound like my jurisdiction."

"Yeah, that's where the kicker is. The M.E. found skin tissue in between her front teeth and when the DNA report came back, it flagged another cold case, but the owner of the DNA is nowhere in the CODIS database, so this guy has never been caught...yet."

"Ah, I see. But, how can I help you, why not call the Atlanta division?"

"That cold case was from 20 years ago, the dissolved body of a husband and Father... remember that one?"

Jake pinched the bridge of his nose with his fingers and shut his eyes. Of course he remembered, that case was one of his first big cases that he was put on when he was a rookie, before he went into the FBI. He had been a beat cop for the Atlanta PD for a few years before moving to detective and he'd only been 27 years old. That case has stuck with him through the years. Every lead he got turned up a dead end. Now here he was, twenty years later, working for the FBI and that case is back, but with another body attached.

"Jake?"

"Yeah, I'm here. Listen Holt, send me what you can and I will see what I can do about getting down there, okay?"

"Great, I'll have everything emailed over within the next ten minutes."

"Thanks. I'll let you know any travel arrangements and all of that, as soon as I get clearance to jump on this case."

"Sounds like a plan. And Jake, thanks. We really need this guy caught."

"I agree. Talk soon Chief."

*****   *****

Jake waited for the email from Chief Montgomery, before he thought about getting permission to grab the new case. All the while he waited, his mind was churning with ideas and one popped to the forefront, one he was leery about bringing up, but if anything could help with this case, she could.

Next thing he knew, he was texting his college buddy, Kris St. Claire.

"Kris, it's Jake. How soon do you think you and Eva could get to Atlanta, GA?"

Eva St. Claire is the idea that popped into mind when he thought how he could close this case. He had sort of retained Eva's talents in another case he had in Kentucky, right before the Derby, and she did amazingly well. Her methods were a little unorthodox, as he had seen first hand, but they worked and that was all that mattered.

His phone dinged with a reply from Kris. *"Why, what's up?"*

Jake went with a quick reply for the moment, until he got the email he was waiting for.

"May need Eva. I'm waiting for more information, so I'll text you soon."

No sooner had he sent the text, he checked his email and there was one from Chief Holt

Montgomery waiting for him, with an attachment. He clicked on the attachment to open it and the file had twelve pages of notes from the M.E. and all of the notes that the officer working the case had taken, too. He saw the name of the officer and smiled. Wade Montgomery. Jake knew that had to be the chief's son, whom Jake hadn't seen since he was born. "Well that apple didn't fall far from the tree."

As he read through the reports and scanned the pictures that he attached, Jake knew it was the same M.O. as his case from twenty years ago.

He took his laptop and headed to his boss's office. Jake tapped on the side of the door, before entering.

"Jake, what's up?"

"I need to go to Atlanta for a few days."

His boss's brows shot up, "Mind telling me why," his boss asked, not so much irritated, but more concerned than anything.

"I'll give you the abridged version. This case that was brought to my attention today, is related to a murder investigation I was lead on when I worked for the Atlanta PD, when I was just starting out. I never closed the case and now this new case has the same DNA evidence that was in my cold case from twenty years ago. A Husband/Father was the victim in my case and I always assumed it was drug related, because he had connections to the Mexican cartel, but I was never able to get the evidence to prove my theory. The new victim however, is a female with no ties to anything really, except she worked for a very elite boat manufacturing company, Atlantic Sea, Inc. She was their office manager and the assistant to the CEO, Alec Brighton.

I've got some time saved up, and I'd really like to be able to take a look at this case, whether in an official capacity or private. Technically, this is a federal case now, since it is connected to another homicide and this is the second one that we know of, with the same M.O."

Jake eyed his boss while he mulled over everything he'd just given him. After what felt like hours, but was actually only a minute, his boss looked up, "I get it, this your achilles heel case, we all have at least one that never leaves us, that always stays at the back of our minds, that we wish we could have solved or maybe done better on." He looked thoughtful for a minute, as if remembering his own cases. "Okay, let me make a few calls to our Atlanta field office and see if I can have you take the lead on this case. I'm not promising anything. They may tell me where I can stick my authority, but I'll appeal to their somewhat sensitive side if I have to."

With a huge sigh of relief, Jake smirked at his boss, "thank you. Anything you can do to get me on this, will be great."

"Yeah Yeah, you owe me Long. Preferably a bottle with a black label on it..."

"You got it!"

Jake started out the door, stopped and turned back to his boss.

"Is there something else?"

"Sir, I may bring Eva and Kris St. Claire in on this case, if I get the okay. Is that going to be a problem?"

Rubbing his forehead, his boss shook his head, "if you think she will be of help, I guess it's fine. I can't say anything bad about her, she delivered on the Kentucky Derby case, however weird that case was, she still caught them."

Jake's mouth tipped up into a small smile, remembering what they went through during that case. Pretending to be her husband, seeing her do her thing and being absolutely scared to death watching it with his own eyes about did him in. After that, he felt very protective of Mrs. Eva St. Claire.

"I'll let you know for sure, probably in the next 10-15 minutes, Jake."

"Thanks, appreciate it."

At his desk, Jake started looking up flights and hotels for Atlanta. He thought about it for a minute, and figured out that it had been at least ten years since his last trip to Atlanta. No sooner had he started scrolling through flight times, that his boss stuck his head out of his office and got Jake's attention. "Jake, you're good to go."

Waving a hand of thanks, Jake continued his search for cheap flights and a place to stay, as well as texting Kris.

"Hey, I just got the okay to work this case in Atlanta. I really need Eva's help. This case is kind of personal for me. I'll explain more later. Thanks."

Chapter Fifteen

While Eva was helping the kids with homework she heard her phone and Kris' phone ding with a notification, simultaneously. She picked up her phone to check the message and internally growled. Kris didn't quite hold in his dismay, as he got the same message.

"Looks like we're going to Atlanta," he said.

Eva put her hand to her forehead and rubbed nervously. "Yep, looks that way. I have to call your Mom. Do you think they'll be okay taking the kids for a few days? Are you going to be able to take off work, again? I didn't even think about that."

"Yeah, it should be fine. I can do 95% of my work via my laptop. And if I have to, I can always go into the Atlanta office. Conveniently enough, most of the work I do is with that office anyway.

I'll make you a deal. I'll call my parents and get that all situated, if you get online and get our flights made."

"Okay, I can do that. I guess it's a good thing that I quit my job at the salon after we came back from Louisville, huh?"

"Absolutely. If we keep getting called out by Jake, I may quit my job," he laughed.

The kids got out of their seats and started running around the kitchen, singing, "we get to go to Grandma's!"

Eva rained on their parade real quick, "you still have to do homework and obey the rules."

The two smaller faces fell, "you're a buzzkill Mom," groaned the oldest.

She couldn't help but laugh, and that got her the stink eye from both kids, as they left to go to their rooms. Kris yelled after them, "start packing clothes and stuff that you want to take to grandma and grandpa's."

Looking online at the travel sites, Eva typed in her query and scrolled through the options available. This would be her first time going to Atlanta. "Do you know what part of Atlanta I should look for a hotel," she asked Kris.

"Let me text him real quick. You may be able to get a better deal if we do air/hotel together."

"Ask him if we need a car, too while you're at it."

*****   *****

Jake walked through his apartment that he kept in Columbus, Ohio, down by the arena district. It was a convenient location, close to the airport, his main office and Nationwide Arena, where he liked to catch a Blue Jackets game when he could. He started packing for yet another case. He pulled out a couple of suits from his closet that still had the plastic bags from the dry cleaner on them and put them in his garment bag, along with a few different neckties and dress shirts, when his phone pinged with a text.

"Hey Jake, is there a specific hotel or location around Atlanta we should be making reservations for, and will we need a car?"

Jake checked the details of his itinerary that he made before he left the office, so he could forward it to Kris. He made it so that they would all be staying at the same place, which was a cool lake house, and texted everything to him.

He was thankful they were being accommodating, so far, when he's asked them to help on cases. Jake also appreciated the fact that he still has that connection to his friend from college, since after he graduated, he'd gone off to Atlanta and worked for a few years with the Atlanta PD and knew no one. That's where he met the now Chief of Police, Holt Montgomery. They were the first ones on the scene of the skeletal remains that had been found in Lake Lanier 20 years ago. That case ended up being the bane of his existence...the one case he has yet to solve, until now. "This person is back for a reason, and they're not going to get away from me, this time."

     *****   *****

Kris was just saying his goodbyes to his Mom when he heard a beep in his ear. A new text message from Jake, no doubt. "Hey Mom, I have to get going, but thanks for taking the kids for a few days. We'll bring them over tomorrow. I'm not sure if it'll be before or after school yet. It will depend on what flights Eva is able to get to Atlanta."

After disconnecting the call with his mom, Kris pulled up the text from Jake.

"We will be staying at a Lake House on Lake Lanier that I secured. I thought it would be nicer than a hotel and it's closer to the site where the remains were found. As for a car, let me know when your flights are and I'll make sure to pick you guys up. If you need anything else, let me know."

"Wow, swanky," Kris said, aloud.

"What's swanky? And where did you come up with that word, anyway," Eva asked, making him flinch.

"Jeez, can I put a bell on you or something? You nearly gave me a heart attack."

"Ha. Sorry dear, I didn't mean to scare you. Did you get anything else from Jake?"

"Yes, that's what I was saying was "swanky", he used air quotes, as began to tell her. "He said we will all be staying at a Lake house on Lake Lanier, since it is closer to the site. He also wants to know when our flights are, have you made them yet?"

"No, I was waiting to see if we needed to get a hotel and car rental, first. I guess I can go ahead and make the flight arrangements now. Do we need a car?"

"No. He wants me to text him our flight number and time of arrival, and he'll pick us up."

"Oh, okay. I will make our arrangements and text everything over to him."

Eva found a flight leaving out of Columbus that wouldn't be taking off until the next evening. She put in their information and payment and sent a copy via text on to Jake, so he would know when they would arrive. She was a little relieved that she would have most of the day tomorrow to get some things done before leaving. If she was being truthful, she needed that extra time to come to grips with what she was about to be doing, yet again. She prayed to God, she wouldn't have any nightmares with her mother starring in them, while she was there, this time.

The previous case she worked on with Jake, had her pretending to be his wife, and they had to stay in the same room and go about everyday life like they were married. It was a little daunting, since she wasn't an actor by trade. They managed okay, and they came out of the whole ordeal knowing more about each other, and she would like to think, as closer friends, too. She knew Jake was a good man, and she respects what he does for a living. Eva didn't think she could do what he does, day in and day out though. It would definitely weigh on your psyche.

After she sent off the text to Jake, Eva headed upstairs to look through her closet and began grabbing stuff to take with them. She grabbed her larger suitcase, because she knew she wouldn't be able to put some of her extra items in a carry-on and get through the TSA. One item in particular, her family's spell book and the ring that was her grandmother's were going in her carry-on, but the vial of pig's blood she doubted would make it through. The other ingredients that she might need, she would buy once they were there.

"Wait, I can't put pig's blood in with our clothes," she mumbled. "No, that won't work. I'll have to put it in my carry-on and spell it to conceal the contents I don't want seen. Oh boy, if people knew I could do this, I'd be in so much trouble." Shaking her head and letting a little giggle escape, she went about packing her backpack and then spoke the incantation in a whisper, "You see these items not, for they are but a shadow." Eva repeated it two more times before zipping her backpack closed.

Turning back to her closet, she stood with her one hand propped on her hip and the other hand under her chin, "Hmm, I wonder what the weather is like in Atlanta, this time of year?" She said it out loud to herself, but an answer came from the doorway.

"Jake said the weather is supposed to be decent, around 70 degrees and sunny during the day, but chillier at night, so we'll have to pack a little of both types of clothes."

"Sheesh, where the crap did you come from? I didn't even hear you in the hallway."

And that thought nearly knocked her on her butt. That just showed how nervous she really is about doing this again.

"Sorry, I'll announce my presence as I'm walking through the house from now on, so you know my proximity."

"Is that sarcasm? That sounds a lot like sarcasm." Eva didn't know where the hostility was coming from, but it was spewing out of her faster than she could stop it.

"No, but paybacks are sometimes a cruel joke. Are you okay?" Kris gave her a look of concern.

"Sorry, I guess I am a little on edge, being that I'm walking into another murder investigation, again. I don't think I'll ever get used to it.

Kris pulled her into his arms and held her close, "hey, I can call Jake and tell him to forget it, you're not doing anymore and to lose our numbers."

"No, then I'd feel guilty. If I have to use my curse, at least I can use it for good." Eva released her arms from her husband, looked up at him, "thanks for giving me the option though," she said, standing on her tiptoes giving him a quick kiss. "Now, let me finish packing."

Chapter Sixteen

Diego made it a point in his business, that he would watch and follow the carriers that would take the boats from Atlantic Sea, Inc. to the port in Savannah and make sure that those boats going on the cargo ships made their way without incident. Today was one of those days. Grant it, he was a little more on alert than he usually was, especially after finding out Alec's assistant found out what they did, but he hoped that wouldn't be an issue anymore.

There were only four boats getting exported this time, but each one had over a million dollars worth of product in each of the steering columns. Before it's distributed to his contact in Cartagena, he will see a nice deposit in his offshore account of ten million dollars, then his man at the port in South America will release it to his seller there, and once he doles it out to his pushers, and they sell it, he should see another nice deposit of five million on top of that.

It's a risky business, but Diego had made many influential contacts over the years, that if he somehow got himself into trouble, he'd be able to get out of it, or get rid of whoever caused him trouble to begin with. Diego had only ever had to deal with one other person who tried to get in his way and that had been over twenty years ago. He had been a young man, just starting out and hadn't yet cultivated his standing in the community. That problem went away and this one will too.

Going down memory lane made Diego smile.

*****   *****

Alec sat back and breathed a long sigh of relief seeing the trucks leaving his warehouse. The nagging thought of what still happened to Marcella plagued his dreams. He didn't remember a thing that happened that night after the bar.

His thoughts were interrupted by a knock on his door. "Come in."

"Sorry to disturb you sir, but there is a man out front asking to speak to you. He says he's with the FBI."

Sitting up straighter, "what does he want?"

"I'm not sure, but I think it has to do with Marcella's disappearance. He said he needed to speak to you."

"Okay fine, I'll come out and get him."

Alec's heart started beating triple time. "Oh dear God, is she really dead," he thought to himself. His legs were shaky at best, as he made his way to his office door.

As soon as he stepped out of his door, the gentleman that was seated in the waiting area immediately stood and made his way over to him. Alec thought to himself, "yep, definitely FBI."

"Mr. Brighton, I'm Special Agent Jake Long with the FBI," he stated, with his hand extended as an introduction.

To his disdain, Alec took the man's proffered hand. "Agent Long, how can I help you?"

"If you don't mind, can we speak in your office?"

"Sure, come with me." Alec walked the short distance to his office, and held the door open for the agent, and once he entered, Alec shut the door behind him.

Rounding his desk and taking a seat, Alec motioned for Jake to sit. "What can I do for you?"

"Well, to start off, I want to extend my deepest condolences on the loss of your employee, Ms. Gallo."

Hands shaking like a Parkinson's patient, Alec took in a breath before speaking. "Marcella's actually dead? And the FBI is involved?"

"I'm sorry, I thought you were aware of her passing."

Feeling bile rise up in his throat, Alec thought he might be sick. "I was told she was missing, but I hadn't yet heard that she'd been found yet,...dead."

Jake looked at the man, trying to gauge his reaction. Either he was truly innocent, or the best actor he's ever seen. He wasn't sure. "Well, that's why I'm here. Apparently you were the last person to be seen with her, so I have questions..."

"I was?" Of course, he figured he was, all things considered, but he didn't think he was the one who killed her, I mean he was told to do as much, but he kept putting it off.

"I was told you and Marcella had been at Regent Cocktail Bar drinking, and things seemed rather awkward between the two of you. Care to explain why that was?"

Noticing the color change in Brighton's face, Jake figured he hit a nerve.

"I don't think it was awkward, but to tell you the truth, I don't exactly remember." Alec went with more truthfulness, than anything, He truly had no recollection of everything that happened that night.

"What do you mean, you don't remember?"

"Why is the FBI involved, and not the Atlanta PD?" It gnarled at Alec's conscience that the FBI was here. Why? " I mean, that's not normal, right?"

"We got involved when evidence suggested the same MO was used in a previous unsolved case twenty years ago. Now, why do you not remember that night?"

An unsolved case matched this one, but how? That had to mean that he didn't kill Marcella, he was off the hook. A small tip of his mouth, that mirrored a smirk caught Jake's attention and not in a good way. "Mr. Brighton, does this new information make you happy about something?"

"What? No!"

"Then why the smirk?" Jake was getting annoyed by the minute with Alec Brighton. *"Smartass rich CEO,"* he thought.

Jeez, how can he get himself out of this one. "Because twenty years ago, I was in high school and didn't kill anyone," was going around in his head. "No, can't say that out loud."

"Sorry, there's no excuse for my smirk. Like I said though, I don't remember a lot about that night," he said stoically. "I guess I drank too much."

"You drank too much? What do you remember about that day, and I mean anything?"

"I remember asking Mar if she would go to the Regent for a drink, so we could talk about a couple of work things."

"Anything else? Did she seem off that day or any day prior to her disappearance? Was she having any issues or problems with anyone that you were aware of?"

"No, Mar was pretty one minded. Her job was her life, from what I gathered. She didn't have a boyfriend or anything."

Jake wasn't completely buying this guy's take on his assistant, but he'd do his own brand of research soon enough. Eva and Kris were set to arrive this evening, and he would go over everything he gathered, with them later.

He noticed Brighton starting to squirm in his chair; he was definitely hiding something. Jake was about to ask him, when the man stood and flat out told him to leave.

"Agent Long, I think we're done here. I have nothing more I can give you. If you have any more questions, I'll give you my Lawyer's number and you can go through him, from now on."

"You realize that makes you look even more guilty of something, right?"

Alec didn't respond, he thought it was better to escort the agent to the door, because he needed to make some calls.

Jake walked to the door, turned and handed Alec his business card. "Call me if you recall anything, and don't leave the state." And with that last parting shot, Jake walked out, leaving Alec Brighton's mouth agape. It was a dick move, but one he felt needed to be out there.

Chapter Seventeen

Jake walked into the Atlanta PD, looking for Chief Montgomery. Looking around the department, he noticed that not much had changed since he was here last. An older gentleman stepped out of the back office, the man looked to be in his late 50s. He was tall, slim and graying at the temples with a salt and pepper mustache, but the gate in the way he was walking toward Jake, brought immediate recognition.

"Hey there old man, can I get any good coffee in this place," Jake teased.

Chief Holt Montgomery looked up, shook his head while grinning from ear to ear and made his way over to Jake. "Keep it up kid, and I'll make you drink the sludge in the break room."

The men hugged, smacking each other on the back. "Jake Long, it has been a minute, hasn't it?

How do you like working in the big leagues, with the FBI?"

"It's not so bad. What's it been, almost twenty years? I saw your last name on the reports I was sent, but the first name threw me at first. Looks like your son is following in your massive footsteps. Being that he is old enough to do so, makes me feel ancient."

"How do you think I feel? Wade is 24 years old. I'll be a grandpa before I know it."

"He's married?" Jake almost envied him. "I haven't even gone down that road yet."

"Not yet. He is engaged to his high school girlfriend though. They've been together for eight years. You're still not married? What are you waiting for?" Chief Montgomery shook his head at the mere thought.

"Waiting to find time to date someone, I guess. The job doesn't lend itself to being a family man." That was always his excuse and that's exactly what it is, an excuse. A lame one at that, but he'd been using it for so long, it was his automatic response.

"Uh huh... Anyway, I'm guessing you have gone over the reports that we sent. Let me grab Wade and see if he has anything new to show you, okay? We'll go into the conference room down the hall there, on the right. You go ahead while I look for him."

"Sounds good Chief," he said, smiling. "Oh yeah, and make sure you bring the good coffee back with you."

Montgomery gave him a one fingered gesture at the request and went in search of his son.

Jake sat at the conference room table, lost in thought when his phone went off. A text notification.

"Hey Jake, so far our flight will be on time, arriving in Atlanta at 7:25pm."

Jake sent Kris a quick message back confirming the arrival time and that he'd see them, then. He hadn't checked into the lake house rental yet, since the check in time wasn't until 4pm, so he dove right into the case as soon as he got to Georgia. He still had a nagging feeling at the base of his brain about CEO Alec Brighton, that was one of the reasons he showed up at Atlantic Sea, Inc., without any warning. He wanted to get a feel for the guy. There was something definitely off about him and his story.

***** *****

Wade Montgomery was parking his patrol car in the parking lot, when his phone started ringing. He put his car in park and grabbed his phone, "Officer Montgomery," he answered.

"Officer Montgomery, this is Francesca Rose, Marcella Gallo's friend."

The urgency in the woman's voice made Wade sit up straighter, "Ms. Rose, how are you holding up?"

"I'm hanging in there, I guess. Any news on who killed Marcella?"

"Not yet, I'm sorry. We are working on it and the FBI has been brought in. Was there another reason you were calling?" He could hear it in her voice, something was off.

"Actually, I might have something for you. I just checked my email, it's been days since I checked it and I should have checked before now, because there was a strange email from Marcella from the day before she went missing."

That got his attention. "Can you forward the email to me, please? I would like to check it out."

"Of course. There are pictures attached, but I'm not sure what I'm looking at. It looks like pictures from the Atlantic Sea warehouse and the boats. There is a man in the picture and I'm not sure what he's doing, but I'll send them over to you, now."

Wade immediately rattled off his email address at the precinct and told her how much he appreciated her calling with this new information and disconnected the call, so he could get into the building and download that email.

He ran like a bat out of hell through the front doors of the station and nearly plowed his father down.

"Whoa, where's the fire boy?"

Breathing heavy, Wade apologized. "Sorry Dad, I have to get to my computer and download an email from Marcella Gallo's friend Francesca. Marcella emailed her the evening before she went missing and the email has pictures in it. I have to see what it is."

"Grab your laptop and bring it to the conference room. Jake Long, who used to work here, is with the FBI now, and he's in there waiting for me, but he will want to see this. He's the one they sent to help with this case."

"Okay, I'll be there in a minute."

Holt marched into the conference room where Jake was seated. "Well, you're not going to believe this. Wade is expecting an email from our victim's friend, Francesca. Marcella apparently sent her an email the night before she went missing, and there are pictures attached. He's bringing his laptop in, and we'll open it in here."

Jake eyebrows rose, "really? That sounds interesting."

Wade ran into the conference room and Chief Montgomery did the introductions, "Wade, this is Special Agent Jake Long; Jake, this is my son, Officer Wade Montgomery."

"Nice to meet you, sir," Wade responded with sincerity.

"You too, Wade. I remember when you were one year old. Wow, time surely does fly." Jake was feeling older by the minute.

"So you worked with my Dad back in the day, huh?"

"Yeah, back in the day..."

"Sorry, I didn't mean anything by that, I'm sure you're younger than him," he said, grinning.

"About ten years younger, thanks."

Getting annoyed with the topic of age, Holt Montgomery stopped the age conversation, "alright, are we going to check out this email or what?"

Jake smirked at Wade, "he's a little touchy about his age, isn't he?"

Wade stifled the laugh that was about to explode from his chest. "A little."

The laptop was set in front of Wade, and he opened his email account and waited for new messages to download. He saw the email from Francesca right at the top, clicked on it and started downloading the images. The two men stood looking over his shoulder, reading the context of the email, which wasn't very much.

"Dear Francesca, I'm sending these images to you, as a backup. Thanks, Mar"

As the images started coming up, the men all stared at the same thing, the image of the boat's steering column being loaded with small bags of white powder.

"Damn, that looks like heroin," Jake said. "Can you make the picture of the guy on the boat any clearer? We're going to have to upload it into facial recognition software."

"I'll see what I can do. These pictures look like they were taken some distance away," Wade responded.

"Do what you can, but I need a printed copy immediately. I'm going back to Atlantic Sea, Inc. to see if I can get some answers out of Alec Brighton. Like who the guy in the picture is."

"The picture should be sitting on the printer in Dad's office."

"Thanks. By the way, I am picking up a couple of people from the airport tonight, who will be assisting me in this case. Do I need to get them any kind of special badge to be able to come into the station with me?" He looked to Chief Montgomery for an answer.

"No, as long as they are with you when they are here, they should be fine. Who are they, extra agents?"

Jake's face gave nothing away when he responded, "not exactly." And with that, he left to grab the picture and headed out.

Chapter Eighteen

Eva and Kris were sitting on the plane, about to land at Hartsfield-Jackson airport in Atlanta. She grabbed her carrying-on bag and looked inside. Her family's book of spells and a couple of special bottles of ingredients were tucked neatly into the bag with her white silk scarf wrapped around them, so when they went through TSA security checkpoints, the items didn't show up as suspicious. She was thankful her little concealment spell had worked.

"How many times are you going to check to make sure your book and everything is still there," Kris asked her, giving her a teasing smile.

She deliberately gave him the stink eye, "as many times as I want. Don't make me turn you into a cockroach."

One eyebrow raised, he looked down at her, "you can't actually do that, can you?"

"Do you really want to find out?" She gave him a sly smirk, then winked at him.

"Everyone, please be seated and fasten your belts as we descend into the Atlanta airport. The temperature in Atlanta is a balmy seventy-two degrees, with moonlit skies," the captain announced.

Eva shoved her carry-on back under her seat and buckled up. "This flight wasn't too bad. I don't even think it was an hour and half long. Of course the glasses of wine helped pass the time, she said, laughing.

"Yeah, it's usually around an hour and twenty minutes." Kris leaned in and asked with humor in voice, "you're not schnockered, are you?"

"No, not at all. I am merely relaxed."

"Uh huh. I already called the office here and let them know that I'd be here, working. I won't be too surprised if they ask me to pop in one day."

"Wait, you're not going to leave me on my own, are you?" Eva knew she was being a little unreasonable, but she was getting a queasy feeling in the pit of her stomach. It wasn't a good feeling.

Of course, it could have been from the wine and being thousands of feet in the air, but who knows.

"I thought you were feeling relaxed? What changed that quickly?"

Kris took her hand in his, turned it over and brought it up to kiss the back of it. "You realize you will probably be the one who is leaving me by myself 90% of the time, right? You will be working with Jake most of the time. I'll help when needed."

"I guess. I just hope he has a better plan than his last hair brained idea. I'm not a good actress, especially when I had to play his wife."

"I think you're a better actress than you think. That was definitely not my favorite week," Kris stated, still a little annoyed by the fact that Eva and Jake had to pretend they were married while working a case.

Eva looked up at him, noticing the change in his demeanor. "Kris St. Claire, were you a little jealous?" She was teasing him, but trying her best to get some sort of smile back on his face.

"Not jealous… worried. Jake is FBI, he lives and works in a dangerous profession and you were in the middle of it and still are. Of course, even before that, you got yourself into some harry predicaments all on your own, didn't you?" Kris gave her a wistful look, remembering how they got started working with Jake in the first place.

"Hey, you're the one who called on your old roommate for help, remember? We owe him, whether we like it or not. He's saved my life, a couple of times now."

Kris gave a low grumble, remembering everything that has happened in the few short months since Eva began using her family gift, again. "Can I ask you one question?"

"Of course, anything. But only one, we're about to land," she smiled.

"Do you regret the first time you used your magic again after so many years?"

Without even thinking about her answer, she blurted out, "not even a little, because if I hadn't, Chrissy would more than likely be in jail for the rest of her life, for something she didn't do. How can I regret saving her from that life? And maybe, just maybe, I've neutralized the threat against me, by capturing and trapping the evil entities that had caused all the problems to begin with."

"Well, how can I argue with that logic?"

"You can't. Now buckle up buttercup, we're landing soon."

With a slight shake of his head, he looked down at his wife, "it's a good thing that you're awfully cute."

"I know," she said with a sparkle in her eye.

Chapter Nineteen

Jake parked his rental in the airport parking garage when he got a text from Kris letting him know that they landed and would meet him at the baggage carousel. "Perfect, I'm right on time."

He entered the massive airport, right where arrivals would be picking up their luggage at one of the twenty carousels. There was a computerized board overhead that listed the flights that recently arrived, so he looked for the one that said Columbus, Ohio and saw that their luggage would be coming down the carousel marked 12.

Walking toward the carousel marked 12, he started feeling nervous all of the sudden. How was he supposed to greet them? The last time he saw Eva and Kris, they were all in Louisville, Kentucky, and he and Eva were undercover, or Eva was more undercover, but they were playing a married couple. Jake really hoped that Kris was over that whole case and would act as if nothing was weird. He wasn't so much worried about Eva, she always seemed to take things in stride. Easy Breezy would be how he would describe her demeanor, for the most part.

"Jake!"

Hearing his name brought him out of his head, and he turned around to see Eva and Kris walking his way. She wore the biggest smile and looked actually happy to see him.

"Hey Jake! We made it. I thought John Glenn International Airport was big. Holy moly, this place is like its own zip code. I mean a subway train to take you from the gates to the baggage area. That's crazy," she said, as she reached for him and gave him a big hug. "Kris told me this place was big, but I didn't really believe that it was on this scale."

Kris stood behind her, laughing, "Sorry man, she had some wine and espresso on the plane." Jake shook Kris' hand, and smiled in understanding. Eva popped him in the shoulder at that remark.

"Ignore him, I'm glad to see you Jake."

Jake wasn't so sure if she would remain so jovial and lovey dovey with him once she saw the case file pictures, but he wasn't going to go there just yet.

"Let's get all of your luggage, and then we'll drive out to the lake house I rented for our time here. I've checked in, essentially, but I still haven't gone out there yet. The property manager gave me the code to get into the front door, so we should be fine."

"Ooh, a lake house, nice. How did you manage that one," Eva asked, quite impressed and happy, especially since she wouldn't have to live out of a hotel room for a week.

"My boss loves me," he laughed.

Kris just chuckled, "so, how long of a drive is it to this lake house?"

"It sits on the southern tip of Lake Lanier, so it will take about forty minutes to get there from here."

Eva sat in the back seat of Jake's rental SUV, staring out the window at the landscape passing her by. The sun was setting and the sky showed a beautiful azure with pinks and oranges strewn throughout, with wispy clouds. The city of Atlanta itself seemed huge and very congested, but the further they drove away from the city though, she noticed that it became less hectic. She noticed a lot of what she assumed were Georgia Pines and magnolia trees along the roads.

When they pulled off the highway, they drove for another twenty minutes, before the GPS told Jake to turn right onto a rugged dirt road. The drive wound its way down and then back up a bit, finally revealing a large open area with a decent size structure sitting on it. There was very little light, by the time they got there, except for the interior lights that the property manager obviously left on. Once they were in front of the house a motion detected light came on, illuminating the whole front side of the house.

They all saw that the house was more of a large A-frame log home, than a typical house. It had a large wrap around porch and a wall of windows facing out at the lake. "This will do," Eva said, with wide eyes and a big smile.

The three of them could definitely live here for a week and not step on each other's toes, that was for sure.

The closer they got, she noticed another building off to the left of the house, a garage with three doors. Eva thought Kris would be in heaven;

actually, any man would be in heaven with that big of a garage space and a lake below, with a dock.

Jake punched in the code for the front door and it opened into a massive living space with at least 20 foot ceilings, dark hardwood floors, a floor to ceiling stone fireplace, a decent size flat screen TV above the mantle and a dark brown leather couch, loveseat and recliner centered around the room. The great room opened into a chef's kitchen with all stainless steel appliances and black quartz countertops and a decent sized island sat in the middle.

"Wow, if the rest is anything like this area, we're moving here. Do you think they'd sell?"

"Eva, this place is probably worth close to a million dollars plus, honey,"

Her mouth dropped open and she just stared at him. "Damn."

She set off to explore the rest of the house and yelled down to Jake, "what bedroom are we assigned to?"

"If you see a room that looks like it could be a master bedroom, take that one."

Eva ventured up to the second floor, peaking into each of the bedrooms. She counted five bedrooms on this floor, and found the largest one at the far end. It consisted of a large king-size sleigh bed, in cherry wood, a beautiful damask comforter and duvet covered it, and the walls were left fairly untouched, except for a few black and white 11x14 photos of the views from around the lake, which covered a portion of the wall above the headboard.

As she walked into the master bathroom, she took stock of the size and sheer beauty that she was looking at. This house was definitely decorated by a professional, she concluded. The black and white tile covering the floor looked like it had just been put down, and the large open shower surrounded by what she thought was river rock, was all open and beside the shower lay a massive soaking tub with jets. A rectangular picture window overlooking the lake and the trees sat above the tub. She made a mental note not to use the tub at night when she would have to have a light on in the bathroom, because who knows who might be out there spying.

"Eva, where are you?"

She heard Kris yelling from the first floor. "I'm in what I assume is the master bedroom, why? What do you need?"

"Jake needs you to come downstairs."

Eva's nose wrinkled, "well, here we go again."

Chapter Twenty

Jake was getting antsy to get on with the investigation. This was his one case that he had not yet solved and now there was a new victim, twenty years later. Who goes dormant for twenty years? So many questions, and no answers. Now that Eva is here, he's hoping that she can do one of her hocus-pocus spells and find something he can work with.

"Hey Jake, Kris said you wanted to talk with me a little."

"Yeah, I wanted to go over the case with you a bit. Actually it could be considered two cases."

She looked at him, sideways. ""I'm sorry, two cases?"

"One case is from almost twenty years ago and was never solved, and this one has the exact same M.O. as that one. It can't be a coincidence. No two people could think of the same sadistic way of killing someone. If you can give me anything on this new one, I can close the one from back then."

"So, no pressure then, is that what you're saying," she stated, a little too sarcastically.

Jake stood in front of this petite woman, whom he had grown quite fond of, and gave her a sly smile.

"Jake Long, don't you give me that smile. I know how you operate, remember? We were technically married for a week. And I learned quite a bit in that short time"

A laugh came from the other room where Kris was setting up some computer equipment.

"What are you laughing at St. Claire?" Jake tried for the tough guy attitude, and failed.

"Not a thing. She's your problem this week."

"I'm right here, and I am not the problem, I am the solution apparently. You need me. Now why don't you tell me about this case, so I can have my panic attack and figure out how to help."

Jake grabbed the files he was given by Chief Montgomery. They included photos from the autopsy, and the M.E. 's cause of death, as well as the files from the case he worked on twenty years ago. He knew this wasn't a coincidence, he just needed Eva to figure out a way to prove it.

He placed everything on the dining table where he could spread them out.

Eva walked over to where Jake was arranging a slew of photos. She took one look and turned the other direction and dry heaved. "Oh my gosh, I'm glad I didn't have much food in my stomach. You could have warned me."

"Sorry, I didn't realize you were right behind me. Maybe I should put a bell on you or something." He was teasing her and she knew it,but she gave him a punch to the shoulder anyway, because Kris had said the same thing, not that long ago. He was acting as if she really injured him. "I thought from everything you've seen and done, you would have a stronger stomach than that."

Eva genuinely liked the guy, it was the job she wasn't so thrilled with and when she looked at those pictures of just skeletal remains, it reminded her of why she was actually here.

"Eva, just pretend they're Halloween skeletons."

She looked over his shoulder at the offending pictures, shouldering her gag reflex and sucking in a deep breath.

"Okay, so what am I looking at here? I can tell certain bones, but how old are they?"

"That's the issue, you'd think these bones were at least fifty years old, right?"

"Yeah, but aren't they from the twenty-year-old case?"

"Nope, these bones are from our recent victim, from four days ago. This is Marcella Gallo."

Eva's mouth dropped open, comprehending what actually happened to this woman and the cause of death, which stated it was basically an acid bath, which in turn dissolved all of her skin and muscle, leaving only bones.

"That is pure evil right there."

"Yes, it is. I have always thought that the first one was drug related, because the man did have ties to some drug pushers back then, but I'm not sure about this one. I'm ninety-nine percent sure it has to do with drugs, after seeing the pictures the victim sent her friend. I think she came upon something she shouldn't have and she paid for it. The CEO of Atlantic Sea, Inc. isn't exactly being upfront with me. I want to see if you can come up with a way to do your thing in a couple of different locations.

"Do my thing? You mean my hocus-pocus, mumbo jumbo thing?" The humor in her voice was not lost on Jake, and he gave her a rueful smile.

"Yeah, that thing.

I'm going to see if we can get into the Regent Cocktail Bar after hours, because that is where Alec and Marcella were seen arguing, and then I want to get you over to Alec Brighton's home on Lake Lanier where I know he has a boat. I want you on that boat for sure, because that may be the last place Ms. Gallo was alive, for all I know."

Eva was taking notes, while Jake was explaining the plan. She made a list of possible spells that might work, to get the results Jake was wanting, too.

"Okay, so you want me to do a spell to see the past, like I've done in previous cases, is that it?"

"If you think that is the one that will help, then yes."

"I'm going to need to go shopping first thing in the morning for a few items, the rest are in my backpack."

Jake looked at her with a questioning stare. "What were you able to bring on the plane in your backpack that the TSA let through?"

With a little twinkle in her eye, she gave him her brilliant smile, the one that he was already getting very familiar with, and wasn't sure he was going to like the answer. "Eva..."

Kris came into the living room just as Eva let out a high-pitched laugh. He looked to Eva, with a raised brow, "what did you do?"

"Me? I did nothing you didn't already know about. Jake asked how I got my backpack through the TSA, when it had some items in it that most definitely would not have gone through, otherwise."

"Ah yeah, you better tell him." Kris walked over to his wife, put his arm around her shoulder and nudged her to confess.

"Tell me what? Do I want to know? Is it illegal?"

"That's sort of a gray area, actually," Eva said.

"Oh brother, I don't want to know. Forget I even asked."

"It's not that bad. I needed to bring the pigs blood, because really, where would I find that here, right? I put it in my backpack wrapped in a scarf that had been spelled. So basically it's like it wasn't even in there, that's all. The TSA saw everything, but the scarf and what was wrapped in it."

"That's all!? That's all she says." Jake was pacing back and forth in the dining room, having a minor freak out.

Eva looked up at Kris, "Is he okay?"

"I'm not sure, I've never seen him do this before. You probably shouldn't have told him about the whole spelled scarf thing."

Jake turned around, grabbed his bag and hiked it up the stairs, "I need sleep, I will see you both in the morning."

Kris turned to Eva, "Well you did it, you broke the big bad FBI agent."

Looking flummoxed, Eva put her hands in the air, "What did I do?"

"Nothing, and you did not break the BIG BAD agent, Eva," he yelled down to them.

Kris snickered and Eva shot him the look. "Sorry."

"I'm going to bed after I text your mom and let her know we're here, and ask her how the kids are."

"Are you banning me from the bedroom for that remark, or am I allowed to sleep in the nice comfy bed, too?"

She just shook her head and laughed her way up the stairs.

Chapter Twenty-one

Eva was in a dead sleep, as far as Kris could tell, but there was something in the air that didn't feel right to him. He rolled over and put his hand to her forehead; it was clammy to the touch. "Why was she sweating?"

The black of night made the deep Connecticut woods even more arcane than usual. She knew exactly where she was and where she was heading, it did little to placate her mind though. Eva thought she was finally over having to see her mother again. The evil entity that had tried to inhabit her mother was locked away and nowhere near her.

While Eva continued on her journey down the path, she noticed that even though it was still Fall, the trees and brush all around her continued to look black and dank, dead even. It could be because it was nighttime, with little light from the moon, but she knew that wasn't it. Everything in this area would always be dead to her.

The light from the small fire in the forest's opening grew brighter as she walked. Eva wasn't feeling the dread that was usually associated with seeing her mother, and she wondered why this time was different.

When she reached the small bonfire, no one was there waiting.

"Hello?"

"Eva, my darling granddaughter."

Eva turned around at the voice she recognized immediately.

"Gran, is that you? Where are you?"

A slight rustling of the leaves on the ground drew her attention to the opposite side of the fire. A small figure appeared to be walking toward her. There was a white aura surrounding the tiny woman. Her father's mother had always been small, but one of the strongest women she knew. She was a white witch that worked on the land her whole life, growing vegetables, herbs and the most beautiful flowers you'd ever see. Eva thought of herself more like her grandmother than anyone in her family.

A tear trickled down her cheek at seeing the older lady in front of her. She hadn't seen her since she passed away years ago. Her hair looked just the same as she remembered, long, thick, white and in a very intricate braid, pulled over her shoulder. She was wearing a gray organza sheath dress and her face didn't show her real age; it never did. Eva thought that her gran may have used a bit of magic on that part of her, but she wasn't for sure. She always looked radiantly youthful.

"Gran, what's going on? Why am I here, with you? Usually when I have this dream, my mother shows up to wreak havoc on my life."

"Eva, sit a spell. I wanted to see how my granddaughter was doing. You've had quite the year, haven't you?"

"You know about what I've done this past year? How?"

"Oh Eva, I know all about your life sweetheart. I know you have a wonderful, loving husband and two beautiful children, as well as you suddenly embracing your magic, in order to help the greater good. I am so proud of you dear. Just be very careful, you are more powerful than even you realize."

"What do you mean? You are not the first person to say that to me. Is there something my family is not telling me Gran? I don't want to turn into my mother, I don't want to give into the magic, I really don't, but since the FBI knows I can help in certain ways, they kind of call on me to do what I can, to help."

"Oh Eva, you're nothing like your mother. You don't have to worry about that. You are the purest of witches we've ever seen. Do you not remember the night your mother perished? The power that came over you was more than any of us have ever seen before."

"Of course I remember that night, it was then that I made a promise to myself that I would never practice magic for as long as I lived. You can see how well that turned out, huh?"

"Eva, you can't just stop all magic, it's in your blood. You can ban magic all you want, but it's still inside you. You don't even need to cast spells, because you possess a great magic that resonates from within you. It is part of your soul, dear. No matter how much you dislike your lot in life, it will never go away. Have you not noticed that you make a white light from your energy alone?"

"No, I guess I try to avoid it at all costs. Like I said Gran, I don't want to use it if I don't have to."

"I understand, but there will come a time when you won't have a choice. You will have to use what's inside you, Eva. I needed you to know that it was there, if you ever need it.

This project that you are on now, revolving around the lake in Georgia, you need to be cautious of all that is around that body of water."

"What do you mean? What do I need to be aware of Gran?"

The figure of Eva's Grandmother started to fade into wisps of white mist.

"Gran wait! You have to tell me what to expect here."

Eva turned in full circles around the forest opening, looking for any sign that her grandmother was still there, but it was empty and the fire started to die down where she stood, leaving her in the cold, dark Connecticut forest with more questions than she had answers for.

"Why? Why do the women in my family, the dead ones in particular, pull me into this realm to speak to me, but give me nothing to go on, but subtle clues and riddles. They are worse than a five-year-old. At least a five-year old has never left me feeling completely disconcerted. Well, that's not entirely accurate, I guess."

She turned toward the path she came in from and made her way back to the spot she thought she woke up in. Eva knelt at the location and hoped she would wake up in the bed she fell asleep in.

Kris watched her all night, wanting to shake her awake, but she hadn't looked to be in any distress, unlike some of her other dreams. He'd listened to the quiet noises she made, but none of them made any sense.

She began to toss and turn in her sleep, but wasn't making any horrible noises, so he decided to put his hand to her shoulder and nudge her a little to see what would happen.

"Eva... Eva?"

Eva's eyes popped open wide, and she looked around the room, then back to the man looking down at her now. A little crease showed in his forehead, and she knew she had been dreaming again, and it woke him up. He looked concerned, but not overly; not like the times he'd had to wake her up from her dreams with her mother.

"Hey."

Kris looked her in the eye, "hey yourself. Did you have a bad dream, again?"

"Not really. My mother wasn't in this one, it was my grandmother. She was a white witch, the sweetest woman you'd ever meet. You would have liked her."

"I'm sure I would have. So, this wasn't one of your nightmares that you've had the last couple cases?"

"No. It took me to the same spot in the forest in Connecticut, but other than that, it was nice to see my grandmother again. She did tell me a few things that I wasn't aware of, of course. The women in my family have a strange way of showing me stuff that I never knew I was capable of. I'll tell you about it later. What time is it anyway?"

"It's just a little after 7am. We should probably get up. I heard Jake downstairs already. It sounded like he was making coffee, and I really needed some, because I didn't sleep much after you started having your dream."

"Oh Kris, I am so sorry. I didn't realize I was that vocal or disruptive in my sleep. You could have woken me up, ya know?"

"It's okay. I was afraid if I woke you, you wouldn't find out what you needed to and something bad would happen. Like I said, you didn't seem to be in any distress with this one, so I let it go, but monitored you."

Eva sat up and gave him a kiss on his cheek, "thank you."

"What was that for?"

"For being my guardian, and for loving me, even in my weirdness."

She whipped the covers off and padded to the master bathroom, where she shut the door and left Kris sitting there smiling.

Chapter Twenty-Two

Eva was sitting at the dining room table drinking coffee and contemplating everything her grandma said to her the night before. She'd never heard of this white light energy her gran spoke of, then she vividly remembered that night her mother passed, but she thought it was a fluke that she was able to pull power from her inner self, the way she did that night. Why her, why did she have to have this power? No matter how hard she tried to separate herself from magic, it always came back to bite her in the butt.

She had her laptop open and was doing a search of Lake Lanier. Her grandmother had said something about the lake that made her curious, so she did some digging and was surprised at all the articles and research papers that showed up.

Kris and Jake were talking in the kitchen when she started reading a particular article on the Lake that she thought they would be interested in.

"Hey guys, come in here. You have to hear this. This Lake Lanier is a fairly new lake, did you know that when you lived down here before, Jake?"

The guys both stepped in the dining room, and took seats on either side of Eva. Jake was leaning in toward her screen and reading what she had brought up. "I knew part of the history behind the lake, but I don't know the time frame."

"Okay well, according to this article, Lake Lanier is a man made lake. Did you know that?"

"No, but I do remember hearing it was some sort of government project."

"That's correct. It was built in 1956 by the US Army Corps of Engineers. It was originally made to manage flood control from the Chattahoochee River and to supply water to the residents of Atlanta. Did you know that it is named after Sidney Lanier, a poet and Confederate Army veteran?

According to this, Lake Lanier resides in North Georgia, between Gainesville and Buford. What part of the lake are we at?"

"We are closer to Buford. Atlanta isn't as far from here as it would be if we were in Gainesville.

My victim Marcella, had a lake house not far from here. The CEO of Atlantic Sea Inc. Alec Brighton also has a large house on the lake near here. I picked this cabin for that very reason."

"Whoa, it says this lake was built over several other towns. That's crazy. Oscarville is the more well-known town that used to be here. Oscarville was a small rural town that had been established in 1870, and it was considered an agricultural marvel because the local farmers had fought off the boll weevil infestation that supposedly tormented Georgia from 1915-1990."

"Interesting. Does it mention anything about the deaths that have occurred since the lake has been built."

Eva moved closer to the screen, reading over the article she found. "Here, it says that since 1994, nearly 200 people have died at Lake Lanier, but since its inception, 675 deaths have occurred. That's a lot. This lake is 221 feet deep at the area where the dam is and still 160 feet deep at its lowest point. Holy moly, that would be scary to swim in. There are still forests underwater with trees reaching 60 feet in height and there are other trees, chicken coops, building foundations and cemeteries down there, too. This place is kind of like Atlantis, a whole city underwater."

Kris was drinking coffee and listening to the two go back and forth about the history of the Lake and every thought in his head was sending off alarm bells in his ears. "Maybe we should steer clear of going into the lake."

Jake smirked, "afraid of a little water, St. Claire?"

"No, afraid of what's at the bottom of said lake."

"Well, there are stories of ghosts from the cemetery that still reside at the bottom, that supposedly appear. People that have survived near drownings say that it feels like there are mysterious arms that reach out and try to drag them down under the water. But the creepiest of stories that I read was from 1958, a Ford sedan carrying two women careened off of a bridge and tumbled into Lake Lanier. They say one of the women, dubbed "Lady of the Lake" wanders the bridge at night, in a blue dress, looking lost and restless." Jake gave Eva his deep, scary voice, when telling that story.

Eva felt her face pale and her sight go a bit wonky. "Can we stop talking about arms reaching out and ghosts walking on bridges, please?"

"Yeah, sorry. You are looking a little green, are you okay? You're not going to throw up or pass out, are you? I've seen you go through much worse than just listening to a spooky story Eva."

"I'm fine, Jake. I need food though."

Kris got up and headed to the kitchen, "a toasted bagel with peanut butter, coming right up."

"Perfect! Thank you, sweetie."

Jake just rolled his eyes and shook his head and went into the kitchen to grab more coffee.

"You know Eva, we are going to be going to the rooftop bar that Marcella and her boss were last seen at, later today. You may want to get your backpack and gather whatever items you think you'll need, in case you need to perform one of your spells and whatnot."

"And whatnot," she said under her breath, rolling her eyes.

Chapter Twenty-three

First stop for Jake and Eva was Atlantic Sea, Inc., to question Alec Brighton again, at his office. Jake received some Intel on the man from Jessica Phillips, one of the Columbus office's computer analyst's and Jake needed to rile the man up a little.

"The first time I talked to Mr. Brighton, it didn't go so great, the guy clammed up pretty quickly."

"You think he's got something to hide then?"

"More than likely. I had one of our computer analysts doing some background checks on him and his business, and she sent me some information via email this morning. Time to rattle Brighton's cage a bit."

They pulled into the parking lot and made their way to the front door. There they were greeted by a large muscled security guard, who looked more like a bulldog, with a face only a mother could love.

"How can I help you," the guard barked at them.

Eva flinched, but Jake had his hand at her waist, to let her know he wouldn't let anything bad happen to her.

Jake showed the man his ID, "we're here to see Mr. Brighton. It's official business, so please let him know ASAP, thanks."

Sneering at the two of them, he said, "wait here and I'll see if he is in."

"I already know he's here, I saw his car out front. Now, we can do this the easy way, or the hard way, it makes no difference to me." Jake smiled his million watt smile at the bulldog, letting him know that he wasn't afraid of his size or demeanor, in the least.

The bulldog grunted, or growled, however you want to describe it, and left us waiting at the reception area.

"Is he really here, or did you just take a lucky guess," Eva asked.

"He's here. I saw his Land Rover out front. Jessica gave me all the information on any and all of his cars, boats, motorcycles and ATV's. He has a rather large boat that I really want to take a look at, but can't until I get enough information that will let me get a warrant."

A man was walking toward them looking less than thrilled to see his visitors. Eva leaned toward Jake, "I take it this is the guy."

"Yep, that's him. He's kind of a schmuck, just warning you."

"I have two kids, I'm used to it."

Jake let out a low chuckle, before the man in question reached them.

"Agent Long, why am I not surprised to see you again? And you brought a friend this time. What can I do for you? I thought I told you to contact my lawyer, if you have more questions."

"Brighton... this is my colleague, Eva St. Claire. We have a few more questions regarding Marcella and her last few hours, that we know she was alive. Now, your lawyer wasn't there and you were, so I'm asking you."

They're going to come after me next, with this guy coming back here again and again, I'm a dead man.

"I'm sorry, what did you say?" Eva looked at the man, confused.

Alec shot a look at her. "I didn't say anything."

Eva quickly shut down the remark she was about to make, because what she just heard wasn't said out loud by the man, but it was his thoughts. He was thinking what she heard.

In her head, she merely rolled her eyes, thinking "great, now I can hear people's thoughts, like I didn't have enough weirdness to deal with, now this? It's a good thing I'm used to weird."

Jake pulled her out of her own head by talking a bit louder than he had been a few seconds ago. He was getting to his breaking point with the man, Eva could feel it.

"Brighton, I want you to write down everything you did and said the day that you two argued and I want to know what it was about. I will get a warrant for that boat of yours, as well."

This guy is going to bring death to my door. What the hell am I going to tell him? We argued, we drank, I was supposed to get rid of her, but couldn't and I don't remember anything after that, but waking up on my damn boat the next morning, alone in the middle of the lake. Yeah, he's going to believe that.

Eva gave her head a tiny shake, after hearing him project more of his thoughts.

"I already told you, we went to the Regent Rooftop Bar, we had a disagreement, drank a few too many and I went home. That was the last time I saw her."

"What was the disagreement about?" Jake was losing his patience, quickly.

"I don't even remember."

Eva gave Jake a slight nudge. He looked down at her, and she nodded, letting him know she needed a minute with him.

He took her by the elbow and excused them. They walked just out of earshot, so no one would hear them.

"What's wrong," he asked.

"He didn't kill her."

"What? How do you know?"

"I heard what he was thinking while you were questioning him."

Jake's eyes grew twice their size. "I'm sorry, what did you say?"

Eva winced, "I heard his thoughts."

"Have you always been able to hear people's thoughts?" Jake was trying hard to reign in his shock.

"No, this is something new."

"Ah, and do I want to know what he was thinking?"

"I think we need to go back to the car and I can tell you everything I learned. I don't feel comfortable discussing it here."

"Okay. I need to make a few calls anyway, and we need to go to that rooftop bar and chat with the waitress and the bartender. I want to see if we can go back after hours, and see if there is something you can do with your little gifts."

"My little gifts...you're funny."

"Um, you can't hear my thoughts, can you," he asked, giving her a sly grin.

"Haven't heard anything yet. Are you worried?" Eva laughed as she walked away from him and back toward Alec Brighton.

Jake spoke to the man briefly, reminding him not to try to leave the state, or the country for that matter.

Chapter Twenty-four

Driving through Atlanta traffic nearly gave Eva a heart attack. She noticed that Jake didn't seem to be too phased by it, at all.

"Okay, are you going to tell me what you heard in Alec's thoughts?"

"Oh yeah. Well for one, every time you show up, he thinks someone must be watching his every move and whoever that is, is going to target him and take him out, because they think he's ratting them out to you."

"Interesting. Is this why you think he didn't kill Marcella? Or is there more?"

"He mentioned sort of a sequence of events from that night. It kind of went like, we drank, we argued, I was supposed to get rid of her, but couldn't, and I don't remember anything after that, because I woke up on my boat, in the middle of the lake, by myself.

That's why I don't think he did it."

"We need to get to that bar and see what we can find out from the waitress and the bartender. They had to have noticed something. But before we get there, do we need to stop anywhere to grab supplies for whatever you plan to do?"

She thought about it and went over in her head, the best type of spell that would work in this situation. Eva knew she would have to more than likely go back in time, to that specific night. She wasn't too keen on performing the one spell she had done back in Kentucky, because she had difficulty coming out of it, and it had freaked Jake out more than she'd wanted.

"I was able to bring quite a bit with me, in my backpack. The only thing I would need would be access to water," she said, looking out the window, knowing dang well that this was going to get hairy, again.

"Okay."

Jake looked over at his partner and noticed that she seemed a little distant, or maybe she was just in a zone or something. He really didn't want to ask, asking meant getting personal, and Jake didn't do personal. Of course, he'd acted like he was married to her not that long ago, and that was plenty personal. That was the closest he ever got to being married, and it still made him think what it would be like to have that person to come home to, on a permanent basis.

He was so lost in his own thoughts, he barely heard his phone ringing throughout the car. Eva looked over just as he was being brought out of his thoughts. "You okay?"

"Yeah, I'm good," he stated, before he hit the phone button.

"Jake Long."

"Hey Jake, it's Holt. I just got off the phone with The Regent Rooftop Bar, when are you heading over there? Wade wanted to meet you there, if that's okay."

"We are actually on our way there right now. If he wants to meet us there, tell him to head on over, now."

"Oh, I thought you weren't going until later."

"I want to talk to the waitress and bartender before it gets too busy. I'd like to have their full attention, if you know what I mean."

"Absolutely. Alright, I will send Wade ASAP."

"Sounds good."

"Later Jake. If you need anything, let me know, otherwise I'll hit you up later."

"Later man."

"Who was that?"

"That was Atlanta's Chief of Police, Holt Montgomery and my very first partner, straight out of the Academy. Wade is his son. The apple didn't fall too far from that tree. He's Atlanta PD, too. When I was there, that kid was just born. Talk about making me feel old."

"Age is just a number, Jake. I refuse to give in to the stereotypical age bracket. If you're in your forties, you're pretty much old news. I don't agree. I feel more together now, in my forties, than I did when I was thirty. Besides,didn't you know forty is the new thirty, and fifty is the new thirty-five.?"

"Wait, fifty is thirty-five? I thought fifty was the new forty?"

He flashed a perfect set of white teeth at her, trying not to laugh, but failing miserably.

Eva gave him a lip curl that only Kris knew not to mess with. "Jake Long, are you laughing at me?"

The man straightened up and felt like he'd just been scolded by his mother, "I would never laugh - At you-, I was laughing at the subject as a whole."

"Uh Huh...that perfect smile of yours doesn't work on me, buddy."

She was giving him a hard time, but that dang smile always knocked her off kilter. He really needed a woman in his life. Eva thought about making it her mission to find him one.

Chapter Twenty-five

Atlanta

Eva couldn't get over how big and busy Atlanta was. They were bumper to bumper driving through the city before they got to the rooftop bar. Columbus, Ohio could be busy, but they had nothing on Atlanta, Georgia.

"Was traffic this crazy when you lived here years ago? I don't think I could drive in this on a daily basis."

"We are in one of the biggest and most populated cities. Traffic has always, and will always be crap, but we are only one block from the Regent Rooftop bar, so it's almost over."

"Do you miss living down here? I mean, I know you're from the north, like we are, but would you ever move back.

Jake took a moment to think about her question. "I miss the easy winters of the South, but I don't really miss the traffic.

Here we are, The Regent Rooftop Bar. Are you ready? Don't worry, you won't be doing anything now; we will come back after hours, and we will have the place to ourselves, where you can do your "hocus-pocus" thing."

"My hocus-pocus is what seems to help you solve crimes, I wouldn't be too cavalier about it," she laughed. It was a nervous laugh, but a laugh all the same. Eva was getting a bit more comfortable with her magic, but it still set her nerves racing.

They entered the building and found a sign directing them to the elevator, where they would head up to the top floor, which is where the bar was located.

Neither one said two words while the elevator ascended.

Once the elevator arrived and the doors opened, Eva was assailed by a multitude of different sights, sounds and smells coming from the place. She grabbed onto Jake's elbow and held him still.

Jake gave her an alarmed look and bent down closer to her ear, "what's wrong, are you okay?"

Eva closed her eyes tight, trying to compartmentalize each sensation being thrown at her. Not once has she ever felt this attack on her senses. She concentrated on her breathing and opened her eyes to see Jake's intense gaze. "I'm okay, sorry."

She knew he wasn't buying it, but she didn't have time to worry about it.

"What happened," he pressed.

"It's nothing, I'm fine."

"Eva, don't lie to me."

"I can't explain it. When those elevator doors opened, I was flooded by so many sights, sounds and even smells. I'd never had that happen before. Just give me a second, okay?" She still held onto him, clutching his arm as a lifeline. He held onto the hand that was squeezing his elbow.

"Let me know when you're ready to proceed. We're not in a hurry."

A young man in a police uniform was currently walking toward them. Jake recognized Wade immediately, from meeting him yesterday.

"Wade, how did you beat us here?"

He held out his hand to Jake and Jake took it, "I was already out on call, over by the Coke Museum, so I was nearby." He looked toward Eva, "Hi, I'm Officer Wade Montgomery."

Eva smiled and took his proffered hand, "Nice to meet you, I'm Eva St. Claire, I'm helping Jake on this case."

"Pleasure is all mine, ma'am."

And with that, Eva felt as if she had aged fifteen years.

Leaning in and whispering close to her ear, Jake said, "it's a Southern thing, he's not saying you're old."

Eva took a step back, "how did you know that's what I was thinking?"

"Apparently spending 24/7 with you for a week, taught me a lot about you."

Standing stock still, she had no idea how to respond to that statement. Lucky for her, she didn't have to think about it too long, Officer Montgomery brought her out of her thoughts of Kentucky.

"That's Haven, the one with the bright red hair, standing at the bar. She is the one who waited on Marcella and Alec that night."

"Perfect, let's go chat with her for a bit, then I want to ask the bartender if we can see their security tapes from that night, as well, I noticed cameras outside, as well as inside," Jake said, as he made his way over to Haven.

Wade spoke first, since he had already talked to the young woman. He held out his hand as he neared her, "Haven, good to see you again, how are you?"

"Officer Montgomery, I'm good and you? I see you brought friends with you this time?"

"I'm good. Yes, this is Special Agent Jake Long with the FBI and his partner, Eva St. Claire. They have a few more questions for you on the murder case of Marcella Gallo and the night she and her boss were here."

Both Eva and Jake nodded at the introduction. But neither missed the look of horror on the young girls face after Wade mention it was a murder case, now.

Eva took the young girl's hand, gently "You didn't know that they'd found her?"

Haven shook her head, and then while still holding onto Eva's hand, she felt a zing of electricity at her touch, and she twitched, bringing a look of panic to her face. Eva dropped the girl's hand immediately, but said nothing.

Jake took notice of the inner-action and raised a brow at Eva, to which she gave a quick, barely noticeable nod.

Eva knew Jake would question her later about the incident, but she hoped he'd forget about it. She felt the likeness Haven radiated and believed that she knew what Eva was, because she too, was a type of witch.

Jake intervened saying, "Haven, can we sit and ask you a few questions?"

Still looking a little panicked, she stated, "I've already told Officer Montgomery everything I remember from that night. It was pretty busy, but I remember them both ordering drink after drink, and arguing. That was about it."

"Okay, but did you ever hear anything specific that they may have been saying to each other, a notable word that stuck out in your mind, anything may help."

The young waitress thought about it for a minute. "Not really. Every time I came to take their order or deliver their drinks, they'd both shut down."

Haven let her senses wander, then she felt it, an otherness that she never felt before... Someone in here was special, more special than even she was. Not many witches resided in the South, she knew that. And even her own abilities weren't so powerful. Haven practiced Wicca, but not with a coven or anything like that, but it did make her a little more sensitive to others. It was the woman with the FBI guy, she felt the electricity coming off of her when they shook hands.

Eva felt the waitresses stare, and looked up in time to see her glare right into her eyes, searching. Eva's eyes widened a bit and the waitress shook her head, and looked away.

"Jake, can I talk to you for just a second, please?" She put her hand to his forearm and squeezed.

Jake looked perplexed, then saw the pleading look in her eyes, and excused them to walk away.

"What's up? What's wrong? You've been a little off since we got off the elevator. Are you going to tell me what it is?"

"Haven knows what I am."

Giving her a deadpan look, "how do you know?"

"Because she too, is a witch; not like me, but she has a mild aura of magic around her. I felt it and I saw it. And she knows what I am. I don't think she'll rat me out, because then she'd be telling on herself, too, but there's something there that I can't quite put my hand on. I don't think she has anything to do with this case, but I wanted you to be aware."

"Do you feel that she is a hindrance to this investigation? Will she be a problem?"

"I don't feel anything dark in her , if that's what you mean, but I will keep an eye on her."

"Okay, let's get back to them, I need to talk to the manager now anyway. If you get anything else off of her that you think I should know, don't hesitate to tell me."

"Of course. I'm sorry I dragged you away, but I wanted you to be aware of her."

Taking her hand, Jake whispered, "don't ever apologize to me for something you think I may need to know. We are in this together. You see, and feel things I may not, and your intuition is much better than mine, by far."

Hearing him say that, made Eva smile. "Thanks Jake."

As they walked back over to the bar area, Wade looked up, "all good?"

Jake smiled, "yep, all good. Haven, can we speak to your manager? I need to see if he can bring up the security tape footage for me."

"Yeah, let me go get him," she said, looking relieved to be done with them.

A gentleman, maybe six feet tall, slender build, with a buzz cut that showed hints of gray at the temples came out from behind the bar to greet them, "hey guys, how can I help you, I'm Mitch Colburn, the manager here at The Regent."

Jake shook the man's hand, "Mr. Colburn, I'm Special Agent Jake Long with the FBI, this is my colleague, Eva St. Claire, and I believe you've already met Officer Montgomery here. We are wondering if we would be able to take a look at your security tapes from the Friday before last? We want to see the tapes timed between 7pm and midnight."

"Can you tell me what this is about?"

Wade spoke to the man, "you heard about the woman they found at the bottom of Lake Lanier this past week, right?"

"Yeah, what does that have to do with this place?"

"This is the last place she was seen, before she went missing, and we want to get a timeline and see if we can get any footage of her. We know she was here with her boss, Alec Brighton."

Showing his obvious shock, the manager was silent for a beat before saying, "I saw them, I was working that night. Come with me and I'll see what I can pull up for you."

The three of them fell in line behind the man and went to what looked to be his office. It wasn't a large space, the four of them barely fit. The one wall was lined with monitors showing multiple views of the bar, inside and outside, his desk had a large computer monitor, keyboard and a few personal pictures on it, but that was about it. The far wall housed a four drawer filing cabinet that had definitely seen better days, and the only piece of art that adorned the walls was a 11x17 framed picture of the bar in its earlier days.

Mitch sat at his computer, typing in a few things and clicking on a file, before the monitors all registered different scenes from what they were just watching.

Eva saw Marcella walk in with the man she met earlier, "there they are, on the bottom right screen."

"I see them. Mitch, can we track their movements inside the bar, now that we have a visual?"

"I'll see what I can do. These cameras are on a thirty-second delay."

"Whatever you can get us, is appreciated. I do have another favor to ask you. Would we be able to come back here after hours? Just Eva and myself. I'd like to get a feel for the area and where they were sitting most of the night." He cleared his throat, giving Eva a knowing look and continued, "I can have my superior ask for permission if that helps."

The bar manager looked reluctant at first, but then conceded, "I can arrange something. Do I need to be here? The main door has an automatic lock system that goes in place after 2am, so when you're done, you don't need a key to look up, it locks on its own."

"I'd prefer that no one else be here. We would need someone to let us in, and then we can take it from there."

"If you can be here before 1:20 am, the bar staff will be gone by 1:30 at the latest, does that work?"

"Perfect, thanks."

"Jake look, they're getting into a heated discussion there; upper left screen. She's saying something to him that he doesn't like, that's for sure. I wish these things had sound on them."

"That would be convenient. What time is it showing there?"

"It says 10:46 pm."

As the guys continued to look at the screen, Eva noticed one of the screens showed two men standing at the bar, and they were eyeing the bartender, and Haven as she waited for drinks to be made. The one man, of Hispanic descent pulled something from his suit jacket pocket and while Haven was talking to another waitress, he slipped a hand over the tray of drinks and dropped something into the glasses.

"Guys!"

All three men looked at her simultaneously.

"Look, bottom middle screen. I just saw the tall guy at the bar drop something into the glasses that are on the tray there. We have to see where that tray goes."

Mitch pulled that camera to the center of the monitors, so they all could watch. They saw Haven turn around, grab the tray that had the two drinks on it, and walk away.

"Where did she go?" Eva searched all the monitors, in a frenzy, then pointed, "there, she's walking toward the outdoor patio."

They all looked at all the monitors and the silence was deafening when they saw where she ended up with the drinks. She handed a drink to Marcella, and the other to Alec.

Jake immediately asked Mitch, "go back to where Eva saw the man slip something into the glasses, while Haven wasn't looking."

Once Mitch found the spot where the men stood next to the bar, he took a closer look, to see if he recognized the men, but he had never seen them before. They were new to him, but it didn't mean that any of the other wait staff wouldn't know who they were. He would definitely be checking with them later, for sure. . And Mitch figured they were there for one reason and one reason only, to do something to that couple.

"I'm sorry, I don't recognize either one of them," he told them.

Jake looked serious, "I need you to email me this file, so I can send it to my analysts and have them run it through facial recognition software." He handed the manager his card that had his email and phone number on it.

Looking toward Wade, Jake said, "if you will continue watching these until the bar closes that night, I'd appreciate it. We have to run and get a few things to bring back with us later, but if you see anything, and I mean anything out of the ordinary concerning the two men and Marcella and Alec, you call me. Got it?"

Wade shook his head, "absolutely. Do you want me to meet you all here later, too?"

They both said with odd alarm, "No!"

Jake caught himself, "sorry, didn't mean to sound rude. We will be able to get done what I want to, just the two of us. I'll fill you in tomorrow if we find anything else.

Mr. Colburn, Eva and I will be back around twenty after one, okay?"

"I'll be here."

Chapter Twenty-six

The ride back to the cabin didn't seem as long as it had earlier, because traffic hadn't been as bad. Jake was quiet for most of the trip, merely giving Eva small talk now and then. She knew he was in deep thought, so she didn't let his silence get to her.

Eva was anxious to see Kris. How was she going to tell him what happened earlier, with hearing Alec Brighton's thoughts and sensing the bar waitress's otherness? Nerves pinged off of her like pinball's off the flappers.

Once Jake parked in front of the cabin, he turned to her, ready to speak. Eva looked up, waiting.

"What's up Jake?"

"Are you going to tell Kris?"

Surprise shown on Eva's face. "I think I should, don't you?"

His lips curved into a sly smile. "Let me tell him, please."

"What? Why do you want to tell him? It should be me."

"Oh come on, I've been thinking of a funny way to bring it up to him the whole way back, and I think I figured out one. Please, let me have this bit of fun, while I can; it so rarely happens."

Eva sat there for once, dumbfounded by his remark, and sad that this was the only fun he had to look forward to. His words had her softening toward him just a little more.

"That's just sad Jake, but fine, I'll let you tell him."

"Thanks Eva," he said, climbing out of the car, a bit faster.

"Wait for me."

She caught up to him, just as Kris opened the front door.

"What is the rush? Is this a race to the bathroom?"

Huffing and puffing, Eva stood on the front porch catching her breath. She wasn't out of shape by any means; she runs after kids every day, but going up against a fit FBI agent, well, that was too much apparently.

"No, Jake was..."

Jake held up a hand to stop her from completing her sentence. "Hey! I'll tell him."

Bent over at the waist, with her hands on her knees, she looked at him and snarled. "Ugh...fine, tell him."

Looking restless, Kris eyed both of them, "tell me what?"

"Let's go in and I'll fill you in on a juicy tidbit about your wife here."

Now looking even more pensive than before, he looked at his wife, "what is he talking about, Eva?"

"It's..."

"You said I could tell him," Jake said, interrupting her in mid speech."

Shaking her head, she waved her hand, letting him continue.

With a devious smile, Jake said, "Okay Kris, you could have at least told me that not even my thoughts were safe around this woman of yours."

Eyebrows raised, Kris looked to his wife for any clue as to what Jake was talking about. "What is he talking about?"

Before she could interject, Jake spoke up, "she can read people's thoughts man. Good thing my thoughts are generally PG, but still."

He knew she couldn't read his thoughts, or anyone else's for that matter, except Alec Brighton's, at least that's what she told him.

"Eva, is that true? Can you read people's thoughts, too?"

"No! Well technically, no, but today was the first time I've had that happen to me. I heard what the guy was thinking, like in his own voice and everything. I swear, I've never been able to hear anyone's thoughts before. And I don't hear yours or Jake's, ever. I don't know what happened or how I am able to hear Alec Brighton's thoughts, but if I could stop it, I would."

She took her husband's hand, "I promise you, I can't hear a word you're thinking."

He believed her, but it nearly leveled him to see her looking at him with such vulnerability in her eyes, but he also had to admit that he was in shock at this new revelation. She wrapped her arms around his waist and held onto him with all of her strength. Kris felt the worry rolling off of her, so he held her tight, and laid a kiss on top of her head.

"I do believe you Eva, I'm not mad or anything. Shocked and taken back, maybe, but not mad at you. I think if you could have read my mind all of these years, we would probably have had many more fights than we have had," he said, laughing into her hair.

She felt his smile and his light teasing, and immediately her anxiety level dropped considerably.

"But...that's not all that is new," she said.

Eva leaned out to look up at Kris. It's now or never, she had to tell him everything that came to her today. Rip it off, just like a band-aid, she thought.

Looking like he wasn't sure he could handle anything else new, he cautiously said to her, "let's hear it. What else have you been able to do?"

"I'm not sure what to call it, actually. I met the waitress at the Regent Bar, and I was able to feel her, not quite otherness, but she is definitely a witch, or she's a practicing Wicca, but she knew I felt it, and she knew what I was, too. It was like she felt me in her head or something, it's hard to explain."

Kris was having some really conflicting emotions with all of this new information. He'd seen the things that Eva could do and knew she was different, but he was also scared for her, not of her, of course. But what could he say?

She was eyeing him with suspicion and anxiety. "Say something! You're freaking me out, Kris."

Pulling her back into his all encompassing hug, he smiled into her hair, "as long as you don't tell me that you're also some kind of goblin, I think I can handle this."

Eva half laughed into his chest. "Deal."

Jake was enjoying the banter between his friends, but he had to get this day back on track and that meant getting Eva ready for whatever it was that she was going to have to do.

"Okay, I hate to break up the love fest, but we need to get your stuff ready for tonight, Eva."

Kris shot a look at Jake, "what's going on tonight?"

"Way to break a mood, Jake," Eva said, as she glared back at him. "It's not that big of a deal Kris; we need to go back to the Regent Rooftop Bar after hours, so I can do a back in time spell. Jake wants to see if we can get a timeline of sorts , of all the events that happened the night that Alec and Marcella were there, and see if I can get a hold on what they may have been arguing about."

Jake noticed the inward wince that Kris tried to hide, but he had to know that he would never let anything happen to Eva. To him, she had even become an integral part of his life, and he wouldn't do anything to jeopardize that. And he was just about to say that when Eva took her husband's hand, "It will be super easy, and I trust Jake with my life.

He will be watching me, and he won't let anything happen to me. Okay?"

Knowing there was nothing he could technically do about it, he conceded. "Is there anything I can help you guys with?"

"Unfortunately, I can't use your help just yet, but if we need it, I will definitely tap you in."

Eva headed for the stairs, "I need to get my things together, and I may take a short nap before we go back out, if that's okay."

"Yeah sure, I need to call into the office and check in with my analyst, Jessica who was doing some background checks, as well as facial recognition on the two guys that showed up on the video feed from the bar.."

Chapter Twenty-Seven

Eva walked into their room and took a deep cleansing breath as she tried to quell her impending anxiety spike. She should be used to performing these spells by now, but even she knew she would never get used to the idea of using her magic, no matter how many times she did a spell.

Pulling out her book, she began looking for a spell that gave her similar results as the one she did inside the horse stall back in Kentucky, but without the residual side effects that happened when she came back from the spell last time. She could still see the look on Jake's face when she finally came to. For a tough FBI Agent, he had the look of devastated horror on his handsome face.

Leafing through the plethora of spells in her family's book, Eva came across a spell that looked promising for what they needed, plus she wouldn't need to buy any extra supplies.

Eva pulled out her cellphone and took a picture of the spell on the page, that way she didn't have to waste time writing it out.

Picking up her backpack, she laid it on the bed, unzipped it and started pulling everything out of it, putting the items she would need to one side. The ingredients she didn't need, she put into her smaller suitcase, for now.

After zipping up the backpack, she sat on the edge of the bed, letting out a long sigh.

"I'm so tired..." She closed her eyes and looked to the ceiling, like that would give her insight. "Okay Gram, if you can hear me, please let this spell work. Watch over Jake and I as we dive head first into whatever this is. I really hope I can see you again; I've got so many questions," she lamented. "How did you know these new gifts or talents would show up, now of all times?"

With her head in her hands, she shook her head, and in a whisper she said, "I need a nap."

Eva didn't even bother pulling the covers down, she wasn't planning on sleeping for very long, so she laid down and rolled onto her side, putting both of her hands under her cheek and closed her eyes, willing sleep to take over.

The sun was shining so bright, Eva had to put a hand above her eyes, to shade some of it. She was walking through a small wild flower garden that smelled of lavender, and Sweet Alyssum. She inhaled the pungent fragrance and knew exactly where she was. "Gram's backyard," she whispered to herself, as she continued to walk towards the barn that stood away from the house. She was out in the open now, and if someone was out there, they would definitely see her.

Out of the corner of her eye, she saw movement. Eva immediately went into defense mode, hands out, crouched down ready to pounce.

"Eva! Put your hands down. It's just me darling."

Straightening into an upright position, Eva blew out a long breath, "sorry Gram, I guess I'm a little on edge. Usually when I'm pulled into dreams like this, they're in the forest and it is my mother bringing me there; and those never end well."

"I bet they didn't, but as you can see it's just me, your old grandmother. Come over here, I want to chat with you for a moment."

Walking closer to the flagstone patio in front of the barn where her Grandmother sat on an adirondack chair under an ornate pergola, she maintained her alert senses, and slowly made her way to the extra chair. Looking at her grandmother, she noticed how pretty she looked; even in old age she had beautiful long silver hair that she would wear in a french braid, and she always had it over her shoulder; and her skin always had a radiant glow about it.

Eva's grandmother lived to the grand old age of ninety-eight, and no one would have guessed she was that old. Right now, she was wearing the light blue organza dress that came to her ankles. It was her favorite dress.

"What am I doing here, Gram? Something bad is about to happen, right? Mom used to bring me to the forest and warn me of things that may be on the horizon, and they were never good. Of course, she was still being controlled by the Dagon, at the time."

Her grandmother was about to answer her, when she continued on with her twenty questions.. "But I need to ask you a few questions about the last time you came to me in my dream. You mentioned that I had more power than I even realized. Since then, I have been able to hear the thoughts of a murder suspect, and feel the otherness of a waitress that practices Wicca. Are there any other gifts, as Jake likes to call them, that are going to show themselves? I'm not sure Kris can handle anymore new talents," she said, with a slight grin.

"Oh darling, I know it's been a struggle for you to have to bring this part of your life back. I have to say, you definitely picked a good one, when you found Kris. He loves you very much and I see you've been blessed with two amazing children."

Hearing her grandmother mention her kids, stopped Eva in mid thought. "Gram... Um, I was wondering if you know if...I mean, can you see or can you tell if..." She couldn't get the words out that she wanted to express.

"Eva, don't fret dear, I don't see the gene in either child."

She let out a breath so loud, that her grandmother's eyebrows raised to her hairline, and she let out a small chuckle. "Were you really that worried, Eva?"

Trying to control the intense blush of embarrassment, Eva tried to back peddle her response, but her grandmother held her hand up, "It's okay dear, I understand. You didn't exactly have the best upbringing in this life, and you made the choice to leave it behind and start a new life, I get it. I don't harbor any hurt feelings, trust me. I will always love you and watch over you and your sister.

You have been quite busy over the last few months though, haven't you? What made you open the box, if you don't mind me asking?"

"How did I know you were going to ask that?"

"Go ahead..."

"Okay, you know I swore I'd never practice witchcraft again, and I hadn't, until my boss and friend at the time, was accused of a murder I knew she didn't commit. Unfortunately all the evidence they had, pointed to her, so I kind of took matters into my own hands. I did a back in time spell and saw who had done it, but at the time I had no idea that those behind the murder were trying get to me, because of Mom. I still don't know how they found me, but I fell for it, hook, line and sinker. I thought they had been taken care of, but one was able to

*hang on and well, you know what happened after
Kris' friend, FBI Agent Jake Long figured out what
I was capable of. I kind of work for him, now and
then. I guess if I'm going to use what I've been born
with, I may as well use it for good, right?'*

*Eva's grandmother sat in her chair, as calm as
can be, taking in everything Eva had just dumped
on her. Her facial expression was neither mad, sad
or happy, she just was. Eva looked closer. She
hadn't moved or budged an inch, it was like she was
frozen or suspended in time.*

*She wasn't sure how real her grandmother would
feel, being that this was a dream, but she had her
hand an inch away from her gram's shoulder. Not
sure why her hand was shaking, but was about to
touch her and Gram turned her head and smiled at
Eva and Eva jumped back.*

"I'm still here dear, just thinking."

*"Jeez Gram, you just about gave me a coronary."
Eva sat back in her chair and closed her eyes,
willing her heart rate to slow down.*

*"You need to calm down dear, it isn't healthy to
be that jumpy."*

Shaking her head and rolling her eyes, Eva was at a loss for how to respond. "Gram, I've been through some weird stuff in the last few months and have come close to dying as well as having a dagon try to possess me. So, I'm sorry if I am a little uptight."

"It's understandable sweetheart."

Eva continued, "so why did you bring me here anyway?"

"Oh yes, I almost forgot. I know I told you to expect a few extra things that may be coming and, as you told me, a few have surfaced already. That was just a preview of what you will be able to do. The more you practice the craft, as you seem to have been doing, new things will pop up. I can't pinpoint each ability, because I'm not 100% sure which ones you will have."

"Ulk... can you at least give me an idea of what some of them could be? I don't want to get caught off guard like I was when I heard that man's thoughts. That was a bit disturbing at first. I thought he was saying those things out loud and I asked him to repeat them. Everyone looked at me funny, but I covered it by saying, oh sorry, I thought you said something."

Gram snickered, but sat up straighter, and her face turned more serious. "Eva, I can't begin to understand what you might be going through, but I can tell you this... what you are doing and what you are capable of is something so special, and very rare that this world is far better with you in it."

Eva sat stock still at the enormity of the words her grandmother just said. The pressure it now put on her, made it hard for her to speak for a minute.

"Eva? Eva dear, don't stress and don't overthink it. Your intuition will know what to do and when to do it. Just be careful, and look after Jake, he needs it more than you know. Now, I believe my time is about up. I must go back now, and it's time for you to wake from your nap.

I am so proud of you Eva, you are a wonderful wife, mother and witch." Eva shot her a look of disdain at the word "witch". "Yes, I said witch. It's what you are inside sweetheart. You can't change that. But, keep using it for good, like you said. I love you dear."

She stood and bent down to where Eva sat, and kissed the top of her head, before walking off into the wildflowers.

Eva sat back in her chair and whispered, "I love you too, Gram."

Feeling something touch her shoulder, Eva's eyes popped open, and she looked around. She wasn't outside anymore, and her head was laying on a pillow. As she turned to see where she was, she saw Kris looking down at her, with a sheepish smile. "Did you have a good nap?"

Eva sat up, "yeah, I guess. I must have been dreaming again, my grandmother came to me in my dream, once again. I miss her."

Kris gave her a stoic look. "Is this your mother's mom, or your father's?"

"My father's mother. You would have liked her. She definitely likes you," she added with a smile.

Looking more confused, Kris said, "she had never met me."

"She knows you, trust me."

"That is concerning," Kris said, under his breath.

Eva laughed and climbed off the bed, reaching out for him, and kissed him quickly on the lips.

"Hey you two, none that while I'm sharing this house with you," Jake walked by and joked. "Are you going to be ready to head out in about an hour, Eva?

"Yep, I have everything that I need to take with us. Have you guys eaten anything? I'm starving. I think I'll make some sandwiches before we go," she said as she gracefully left the room.

"She's nervous," Jake stated.

"So am I," Kris said, giving Jake a look.

"I promise you, I won't let anything happen to her. I'll protect her with my life, you know that, right?"

"Yeah, I know."

Chapter Twenty-eight

Jake and Eva reached the bar right on time. The employees were coming out the door, when they pulled up. Haven noticed them exiting their car, and gave Eva an imperceptible nod from where she stood by her own car. She wasn't sure what that was supposed to mean, but she nodded back, but kept close to Jake, as they made their way inside to find Mitch.

They found him behind the bar cleaning up, and sliding the glasses into their slots. He kept a really clean and neat looking bar. The view from the patio area looked amazing, even at this time of night. Eva thought if they weren't on the hunt for a killer, she would definitely hang out here and have a drink or two.

"Do you guys need me to do anything before I leave you to it?"

Jake shook his head, "I think we're good, thanks for letting us have a look while no one is here. We really appreciate this."

"Hey, anything I can do to help. My old man was murdered twenty years ago in a similar manner, and they still haven't solved his murder."

Eyes wide, Jake asked "What was his name?"

"John Colburn, why?"

Jake felt his stomach bottom out and tried to keep the pain out of his face. He couldn't believe it; of all people, this guy's father would be the one case he hadn't solved...yet.

"I promise you, we will catch whoever did this." Jake's voice held more conviction than he meant to convey, but it was God's honest truth. He would bring this person to justice, if it's the last thing he ever did.

"I like your attitude man. So, I am going to head out now. Like I told you before, you don't need a key to exit, I have a lock system that immediately locks the door when you leave, and the security system will turn itself on, as well. If you need anything, you have my number. Good luck, I hope you find what you're looking for."

Jake looked around the interior of the bar a little before walking Eva out to the patio area. She let her eyes take everything in. Walking to the edge, she looked out over the horizon, and took in the beautiful clear night; the moon was just a sliver, so the stars were shining bright, and all the constellations were present.

She took a few cleansing breaths and let her eyes close, so she could feel everything around her. Eva knew Jake was in her space before she opened her eyes. He hadn't touched her or anything, but he seemed to be contemplating a lot. And she knew exactly what he was thinking.

"You just got another reason to solve this case, didn't you?"

He locked eyes with her, "How..."

"It was Mitch's Dad's murder that you didn't solve, wasn't it? And the same person who killed Marcella, is the same one who killed his dad, am I right?"

Jake winched, "yeah, it is. What are the odds?"

"Apparently better than what we would have thought. Are you ready for me to start, or did you want to check anything else out before I do my thing," she smiled.

"Let's do this," he said.

"Alright then, here we go."

Eva was taking items out of her backpack, one by one. The protection spell will be done first, before she does anything else. Pulling her white silk scarf out, she wrapped it around her shoulders, then made a circle out of the white salt, and then she proceeded to place four pillar candles around it at equal distances before she lit them.

She looked over at Jake and winked, "let's get this party started."

Holding her hands out to her side, she stepped into the middle of the circle and began the incantation.

A spell of safety here I cast, a ward of might to hold me fast.

A shield before me and behind, to right and left protection bind.

To me and Jake may no ill will come neigh, but only rede I cry!

So mote it be

Jake looked on as she spoke out loud. Sending up his own prayer that everything would work out.

Eva noticed him standing off to the side, quiet and reserved. She knew that he put his trust in her to do what she can do, and that was all she needed to continue .

"Okay, so the protection spell is set, now I'll set up the other one."

She gathered her supplies for the back in time spell. For this one, she's using pigs blood, salt, baking soda, and two black pillar candles. Eva turned to Jake and asked him to fill a stainless steel bowl with cold water from the bar.

As she poured the pigs blood into a small circle on the patio near the table where Marcella and Alec had been sitting that night, she felt the air around her shift, but didn't think too much of it. Jake brought the water bowl over to her, noting the slight change in her demeanor. "Everything okay?"

"Yeah, I'm just wondering if we're going to get some weather soon? Can you check online to see if we're going to get any rain, anytime soon?"

"Yeah sure."

While he was doing that, she continued with her set up, putting the bowl into the middle of the circle, adding the salt to the water and putting a few sprinkles of the baking soda in four places around the blood, then placing a pillar on top of each spot where the baking soda was placed.

"Right now, I don't see anything out there, so you should be good."

"Okay great. I'm going to go ahead and get the show on the road. Don't worry, you don't have to do anything with this one," she said, giving him a slight smile. He gave her a tight smile back.

Eva stood outside the circle of blood; she had a small piece of paper with the date and time, as well as the location they were at now, written down and started reciting the spell.

Hear these words, hear the rhyme, heed the hope within my mind.

Send me back to where I'll find what I wish in place and time.

Through rite and rout take me to the past I wish to find,

The date, the time and location I've written down.

Let me see what I seek, and return to the present unharmed.

The air surrounding them began to swirl with color, and Jake took a step back from where he was. Feeling nervous, he stood where he was, but he was on alert, in case this went sideways real quick.

Eva had her eyes closed while she said the incantation and slowly opened them to see the swirl of air twist in colors of blue and yellow, but as she looked down at the bowl of water, it too was making a swirling movement, and she saw that a picture begin to form in the water, like a movie playing. She paid close attention to what was forming.

A movie of sorts was playing out in front of her. She saw Marcella and Alec sitting at the exact spot she was at, and they were deep in conversation. It was like a silent movie, until she bent closer to the bowl and sounds started to reverberate off the water. It wasn't loud, but she could definitely hear what they were saying now. They were arguing about something Marcella saw at the plant, and Alec was warning her to let it go, or else. "Or else what," Eva thought. She already knew that he hadn't been the one to kill her. Eva strained to hear everything they were saying, so she moved closer to the ground where the movie played out and everything turned inside out. Eva was now inside the movie with the couple. Looking around, she could see everyone in the bar as if she was also a patron that night. "Whoa, what just happened?"

Eva walked closer to the couple, and waved her hand in front of them, just double checking that they couldn't actually see her. "Nope, I'm completely invisible."

Since it seemed as though she could walk about, she did just that and located the two men that were at the bar that Jake suspected of dosing the two that night. Haven was at the bar putting in their order and not paying a bit of attention to them. The taller man, who was of Latin or Spanish descent, whispered to the shorter one, "she's not looking, do it now." He slyly emptied two tiny vials of powder into both glasses that were sitting on the waiting tray. Neither the waitress, nor the bartender noticed anything. They were slammed at this time of night, she could see that. There wasn't a single open seat anywhere, and everyone wanted their drinks.

Haven finally grabbed her order, and Eva followed her over to where Marcella and Alec sat, and she placed the drinks in front of them. They both gave her a look of disgust, but Haven ignored them, and went about her business, with a smile on her face. Good for her.

She watched the two as they threw back their latest drink. They were utterly clueless as to what was about to happen. Eva waited and watched for a few more minutes from where she was. The two continued staring daggers at each other, when Marcella broke the awkward silence. "I can't believe you let that go on at your company. How much are they paying you? Is it money or drugs that you get as payment... or is it both? I can't work for a company that lets that happen, Alec, I won't. I quit as of right now. You're lucky I haven't gone to the police yet. I told you, either you tell them or I will. What's it going to be?"

He continued to stare at her, his face showing the rage that bubbled inside of him. In less than a minute his facial features began to soften. Smiling, Alec brought his hand up to her face and cupped her cheek, in what would be a loving way, normally, but Eva wondered what he was about to say. She leaned in closer taking everything in. Marcella appeared surprised at first, by the light touch, then she looked resigned. The drugs were starting to spread into her system, too.

"Mar, let's get out of here and go talk somewhere else."

She nodded her head in agreement, going more and more limp.

Alec stood and wobbled a little trying to catch his footing. He held a hand out to Marcella, and she took it. Her balance was definitely off. Eva wondered how the two even made their way to the car on their own. She soon saw just how they managed it, and it wasn't on their own.

The two men that had been at the bar, had been watching the whole scene play out from where they stood, and they were now in hot pursuit of the two, as they took note of the couple leaving.

Eva followed them as the invisible bystander.

Once they made their way down to the ground level, the two were barely hanging on, and after they got off the elevator each suspect took one of them by the arm, and steered them to Alec's SUV and buckled them in, but not before Eva overheard the tall one speaking to the other, saying that they were heading to Alec's home on Lake Lanier, and for the other to follow him there.

"Crap! So, we are far from knowing everything, yet. I'm going to have to go to Alec's house now. I should have known this was going to get more complicated.

I better make my way back up to Jake, he's probably getting antsy."

Eva jumped back onto the elevator and somehow she was able to make it go back up to where the rooftop bar was and Jake stood waiting. She got off the elevator and walked over to where she originally started the spell, and stated her desire to return to the present time.

The air began to swirl once again, and sparks flew, making her jump, distracting her from what her end goal was, which was to get back to the present time. Her head began feeling woozy and her legs shook where she stood. "Get a grip Eva," she told herself.

Willing herself to focus, she let her eyes close for a minute while getting control of herself, and concentrating solely on her breathing. She breathed in counting to five and exhaled slowly, counting to five. She didn't panic, because that wouldn't do her any good, and she knew that, from previous accounts. Not wanting Jake to freak out was her main thought.

*****   *****

Jake stood where he could keep an eye on Eva. Other than some mild movements in her arms and legs, she seemed to be doing fine. He maintained his alertness, just in case anything changed. He looked at his watch and noticed that she'd been under for almost ten minutes now. Hoping that she was finding what they needed, he felt a twinge of guilt in his heart at putting her in the situation at all, but he knew there was no way he would be able to figure this one out on his own. He needed her, and that bothered him more than anything.

He continued to watch over her, when she began twitching more erratically, and that put him on full alert. Moving closer to her, he watched for signs of distress, but noticed nothing too out of the scope of what he'd seen her do previously.

"Come on Eva, you can do this. I know you can come out of this without any problems. I've seen you do it before. I don't know if you can hear me, but please be safe coming back."

*****   *****

Concentrating on her breathing, she heard a faint sound. She opened her eyes and saw that Jake was closer to her body than he had been before. She wondered what he saw to make him close in on her. His stance alone caught her off guard and made her nerves tingle. She couldn't look at him, she needed to get herself back to the here and now.

Talking to herself, she tried to calm herself enough to repeat the words that would get her back.

She didn't want to burden Jake again with that task, because of what happened in Kentucky.

A bright spark of light came through the swirling wind that now engulfed her. She stared into the light and walked toward it. Even though her legs were wobbly, she forced them to move. The closer she got to the light, she heard Jake's voice louder, and that's what she concentrated on.

*****   *****

Jake longed to shake her out of her trance or whatever it was she was in, but thought better of it. He watched and waited for any signs of other movement that may come from her.

He saw her legs beginning to move, and her arms stretched out in front of her; something was about to happen, he could feel it. The air surrounding him was changing. Without even thinking, he moved closer to her, watching, waiting, and of all things, he found himself praying, yet again.

A light began to emanate from where she stood. "Where the hell did that come from?"

Angling himself to see her face, he unconsciously called out to her. "Eva! Eva, can you hear me? I'm right here waiting for you. I can tell something is happening. I hope you're on your way back to me."

Her head flinched slightly. Did she just hear him? He pondered that for a second, and continued talking to her, hoping that it would pull her back to him.

"That's right Eva, I know you heard me, just now. Keep your mind on my voice, if you can and walk or whatever it is you need to do, to get back here, okay? Kris will kick my ever loving behind if I don't get you back to him in one piece, tonight." He let out a short laugh, saying that out loud.

He saw her mouth tip up into the smallest of smiles. She heard him alright. "You think that's funny that your husband would try to kick my butt, if I let anything happen to you, huh?

Okay, if that's what it takes to get you to be here again, then do it, but could you do it a little faster, please, I'm feeling very uneasy here."

Eva's hands shot out in front of her, and the swirl of colored air moved out, nearly knocking Jake on his butt.

Doing everything he could to stay upright, Jake balanced himself, stood up straighter, and waited. The wind slowed and began to dissipate in front of him. Once it was fully gone, and the air was once again clear, Eva stood statue still. The worry seeped into Jake more than he was comfortable with. He inched closer to her, then she dropped straight down to the hard ground, stealing his breath away.

"Jesus, Eva!"
Jake got to his knees and touched her face gently with one hand, while the other checked her pulse, but not wanting to alarm her. "Eva, wake up. You're back, but I need you to open your eyes now, okay."

Jake's heart was suddenly pounding in his ears, and his blood pressure shot through the roof. "Okay Eva, I know you want to see Kris do some butt kicking, but this is definitely now the way to go about it. Please wake up. I need you to wake up."

He was pushing her hair back away from her face. She looked so fragile to him, just laying there motionless, bringing out all the protective instincts in him, again. She promised him she wouldn't freak him out again, like she had in Louisville. Guilt was a horrible feeling, and he was currently feeling it in spades.

*****   *****

Eva felt his hand first, then the desperation in his voice. She'd gone and scared him again. She promised she wouldn't do that. He was going to be mighty upset with her, for sure.

She felt like she was under water, flailing to get to the surface, to breathe in that first large intake of air.

"I'm trying Jake, I'm getting there, I swear. I'm fine, don't be mad at me. I can hear you and I can feel you." Why she wasn't physically moving, she still hadn't figured that out. Damn it, why does this continue to happen?"

She was trying to force any kind of movement from her limbs. They felt like hundred pound weights hanging from each one. Moving was going to be almost impossible at this point, she thought. "Focus Eva, you can do it."

Hearing a grunt escape from her mouth, she felt the smallest of movements from her fingers. "Yes, that's it Eva, move those fingers."

He must have noticed her movement too, because she felt his hands touch hers, and he started making massaging movements on her hand, like he thought they were asleep or something. Maybe that's what she needed. The more he did that, the more feeling she was getting in her hands. She could tell by the way he was talking to her that he could see more movement in her limbs, too.

"That's it Eva, keep moving. Can you open your eyes for me?" There was definite pleading in his tone.

Try as she might, she couldn't budge her eyes. "What is the deal," she thought to herself.

She made her leg move infinitesimally, but it did move, she felt it and so did Jake.

"That's it, let's move some more Eva." He was cheering her on, she could hear it, in his voice.

She had had enough, she was stronger than this. Granted, she figured she may have used up a great deal of her energy with the spell she had done, but not so much that she couldn't wake her butt up. Now more determined than ever, she channeled what energy she did have left, and felt her strength waning, but continued to ignore it. She heard the grunt come from deep within herself, and pushed it farther, continuing to make guttural noises. Whether he could hear her or not was none of her concern at the present moment.

A string of light emanated from her core, and a loud scream came from within as she burst free from the spell, once and for all. It was so powerful, she briefly saw Jake get pushed back a good five feet from where she sat up. Tears were streaming down her face, as she tried catching her breath. Eva rolled to her side into a fetal position, continuing to sob from the sudden exhaustion and emotional overload that she'd put herself through, channeling the last bit of energy she had left. She barely heard the shuffling sounds of Jake moving to her side. He knelt over her, his hands and arms trying to get under her, in an attempt to cradle, and console her.

"Shh, it's okay Eva. You're safe now, I've got you."

Inside Jake was cursing himself a blue streak. He couldn't keep asking her to do this. He didn't want to be the one responsible for her demise or injury someday, because that would kill him, if Kris didn't kill him first.

"Eva, look at me." Her eyes fluttered open and the look she gave him nearly made him come undone. Thankfully her breathing was evening out, and her heart shattering cries had ceased..

"I'm sorry I broke my promise to you Jake," she choked out.

He looked at her completely confused, "what do you mean?"

"I promised not to freak you out again, and I told you this spell would be an easy one," she confessed, trying to smile.

Jake's head dropped to his chest with his eyes closed, he shook his head, fully comprehending her words. "Jeez Eva, it's not your fault, you didn't know. I'm just relieved that you're okay. I can't do this anymore though," he told her.

Eva squirmed her way out of his arms to sit up, and look him straight in the eyes. "You can't do what anymore?"

"This," he spread his arms out over the whole scene. "I can't do this to you anymore. Asking you to perform spells, and putting you in harm's way is the most selfish thing I've ever done, and I'm so sorry."

Eva was mad now, and she stopped him right then and there, "hold on, I wanted to help, this is not your fault, so stop feeling guilty. I've made my peace with this job and if my so-called gifts or talents can be used for good, then I want to use them. My whole life I tried avoiding what I was and I'd been successful at it for twenty years, until I opened the door to my past. You saw what I was and didn't shrink away from it, you called upon it, and made me use it for a better purpose. I'm finally feeling as though I wasn't completely cursed, so don't you dare give up on me, yet. I won't have it!"

How could he argue with her, especially with the severe look she was now giving him. The conviction in her voice made him admire her even more. The thought of her getting hurt though, he wasn't sure he could handle the backlash of that. Jake was at a loss for what to do or say to her.

Seeing that she disconcerted him with her outburst, she held her hand up, "you don't have to say anything, let's just put this behind us and move on, okay? I've got a few things you need to know. For one, we are going to have to do this again, at Alec Brighton's lake house. The two men that drugged them, took them from here, to his house on Lake Lanier. So, suck it up and let's see what our next move is. I have a sneaking suspicion that someone else is pulling the strings here; Thing 1 and Thing 2 are not at the top of the chain on this."

She utterly amazed him, how she bounces back so quickly from things. He stared at her as she pulled herself up to a standing position, looking down at him with a renewed sense of purpose. "Are you for real?"

Eva looked down at him in question, "what are you talking about, am I real? I'm as real as you are. I just find it counterproductive to sit and mope around when there are more important things to be done. Now let's go, we need to regroup, and I'm in need of some ice cream or something sweet.

Oh, and by the way, not a word of this to Kris. You will not tell him about the issue coming back from the spell, got it? He's stressed enough as it is."

"Wait, you're not going to tell him? He'll know just by looking at me, that something went awry."

"Well Jake, don't look like something went wrong. I found out what I could here, now we need to get over to Alec's house and do another one there. Okay?"

Huffing out a loud sigh, he nodded his head at her in agreement. He would try his best to keep a poker face in front of Kris.

They cleaned up the pig's blood, the salt and powder, and blew out the candles, then packed her backpack. They double-checked that the lights were shut off, and the doors to the rooftop outdoor area were closed and locked, then made their way back to Jake's rental car.

The drive back to the cabin was a quiet one, both of them having different things on their mind. Eva was still shaken up by the way she came out of the spell, but she wasn't about to let anyone know that, especially Jake and Kris. She was finally coming to accept that this is what she would be doing and under it all, it actually made her feel like what she did mattered.

Her acting skills were getting better, too. She kept her nonchalant attitude and demeanor in check, so none would be the wiser. No one would be able to tell that she was screaming inside.

Chapter Twenty-nine

The next morning Eva woke up later than she wanted to, and was surprised that the guys let her sleep as late as she did. It was almost 10 am. She rolled to her back and stretched out her legs, then flipped the covers back and padded to the attached bathroom.

Looking into the mirror, she figured out why they let her sleep as late as they did. She looked haggard and like death warmed over. She let out a sigh, and took a brush to her hair to try to tame the Georgia frizz that came with the hot and humid temperatures, but it was of no use. Luckily her hair was long enough to put into a ponytail and wear a baseball hat over that, if the need arose. But first, a shower was in order, then she could deal with everything else that came today.

Eva was determined to sail through the rest of this assignment, with no other incidents to make

Jake question his decision to ask for her help. In her own way, she actually liked what she was doing. It gave her a sense of pride that she was helping to catch the bad guys.

When she was finished with her shower, she didn't even bother with drying her hair, it immediately went up into a ponytail, and she dressed in her khaki shorts, a Nineline t-shirt and her favorite tennis shoes. After swiping on some mascara and lipstick, she headed down to the kitchen to grab a quick bite.

In the kitchen she spotted the coffee pot and someone had already brewed it. "Oh thank you, there is a God," she said as she poured some of the caffeinated magic into a large mug that she picked out of the cupboard. Once she prepared it with a packet of stevia and a bit of half-and-half, she put the mug to her nose and took a deep whiff and closed her eyes. The smell alone of coffee gave Eva a nice jolt, but putting the mug to her lips and taking that first sip was true nirvana.

"I don't know what is going on in your mind right now, but if you're thinking what I think you're thinking Eva St. Claire, you have a dirty mind and I have half a mind to tell Kris."

The intrusion made Eva jerk, spit part of her coffee across the kitchen island and almost lose the rest of the magic liquid down the front of her shirt. "Jake Long! Don't you go sneaking up on me like that, ever again."

He let out a bark of laughter that nearly had him bending in half. "Sorry, but the look on your face was not innocent by any means, woman."

"I like my coffee."

"You were making that face because of the coffee? Wow, I can't even imagine what your face would look like if you were, ya know, thinking about what I thought you were thinking about... never mind," he said, his face turning a pinkish hue. Realizing that he was blushing, he quickly changed the subject. "So anyway, Kris took my rental to his office here, so I put in for another one to be delivered in an hour, so we can go to Alec's house later.

Eva let out a little snicker of a laugh. She found it so amusing that he could get embarrassed so easily.

"What's so funny," he asked.

She tilted her head and shook it at him. "You are. I've never seen you turn so red over something so innocent. It's fun to see something that can ruffle your feathers. Besides, I like that you feel you can joke around with me. It means you're getting more comfortable with me, that you didn't even think before you ripped into me. But then you caught yourself...Don't do that. I want you to feel at ease with me, like a sister or close friend, okay?" She popped him in the arm, and he grabbed it as if she'd truly hurt him.

"You give Kris that kind of punishment, too?"

She wrinkled up her nose and squinted teasingly at him and said, "no, just you." And she walked out of the kitchen.

"Wait! You were doing some research on the Lake Lanier area and its history the other day, right?"

She stopped in mid-stride to turn around, "yeah, I did. The area where the lake is has a lot of history, some not so good. You already know it's considered one of the most haunted lakes, right? I mentioned that before, but the history behind the lake itself is sort of disturbing and extensive."

"How extensive?"

"How long do you have? It's pretty lengthy to explain, but I can give you the nuts and bolts of the history behind it."

"The nuts and bolts?"

"You know what I mean, the bread and butter, the ins and outs..."

"Okay, I get your drift. Tell me about it."

Walking over to the couch in the great room, Eva sat on the brown leather sofa and made herself comfortable. "You might want to sit and get comfy, this may take a minute."

Following her lead, Jake made for the love seat and settled himself in for the long history lesson. "Okay, let's hear it. What is with this lake and the surrounding area? When I worked in Atlanta years ago, I never fully knew the story behind it."

"So Lake Lanier, or (Lake Sidney Lanier) which is its full name, is actually a man-made lake. It was built in 1956 by the US Army Corps of Engineers. Apparently they originally created it to manage flood control and to supply water for the residents in Atlanta. They named it after a poet and Confederate Army Soldier, Sidney Lanier.

"Yeah, yeah, you already told us that part."

"Okay, don't get your boxers in a bunch."

He gave zero retort and motioned her to continue.

" Alright, so several towns occupied the now watery location before they completed it, which I thought was interesting. But when I looked up what the names were of the other towns, it didn't give me anything. The only one they seem to ever mention is Oscarville. So, I looked up why Oscarville was so special."

"And, did you find anything that stood out?"

"I did. A man named Patrick Phillips wrote a book in 2016 about some of the so-called forgotten history of Oscarville. He detailed the 1912 lynchings and riots the ensued after the sexual assault and murder of a young white woman, named Sleety Mae Crow.

Out of fear, about 1100 black residents fled the area to escape the impending violence.

I'm not really feeling that this lake has anything to do with the murder of Marcella Gallo, though. What do you think?"

Jake sat there listening, but also mentally taking notes on other possible angles to look at, and didn't hear the last question she asked. Trying to hide it would do little to help him at this point, so he just replied, "totally."

Eva's brows scrunched together with annoyance. "Totally? Who says that?"

"Sorry, I really was listening, then I started thinking about other possible scenarios on how these two murders that are twenty years apart, happen to coincide, other than from a DNA match."

"Honestly Jake, I think the lake is just a convenience for these two homicides. I'm not feeling that there's any type of connection between the lake itself and the murders, but I'm not dismissing the validity of this lake and it being haunted, there's something going on there, I just can't put my finger on it. I read where a couple of survivors of near drownings say the same thing. They felt hands wrap around their ankles, and start to pull them down. That's not normal.

I know you aren't a great believer in the paranormal..."

"I'm coming around to it, thanks to you," he interrupted.

"Anyway, I know you aren't a full believer, but multiple claims of people hearing bells from one of the sunken churches is iffy, but the other story that really creeped me out was when a Ford sedan carrying two women did a nose dive off of one of the bridges around the lake in 1958 and sunk into the lake, never to be found, and there have multiple sightings after that night of a young woman in a blue dress wandering around the bridge after dark, looking lost and restless, then disappears into thin air, now that's odd. They call her "The Lady of the Lake."

"That was a disturbing story when you told Kris and I yesterday."

"Yeah, but how cool would it be if we ran into her while we're here?"

"You need help. Why would you want to see an apparition?"

"Sweetheart, I had a whole conversation with my dead grandmother last night before we left, nothing shocks me anymore."

"Enough ghost stories.

"Fine. So, what are we going to do once the new rental car gets here, check out Alec Brighton's house?"

"I need to call in to the office first and see if they were able to get any hits on the facial recognition of the two men that drugged Alec and Marcella that night. If we can get names, then I'll be able to have them picked up and I'll question them. If either of them confesses to killing Marcella, then the case is closed. But I get a twitch in my eye, every time things aren't always as they appear and right now I've got twitches in both eyes, so it's not looking good."

"If nothing else, those guys should still be arrested for drugging them, right? You have proof without the spell I did, there's the bar's surveillance. But if there's no facial match, then what? Will you ask Alec if he recognizes them at all?"

"You ask a lot of questions for someone who never wanted to get into this field to begin with, you know that?"

Eva could see he wasn't mad about all of her questions, because he was giving her that little smirk he gives when he's being genuine. She was learning all the faces of FBI Special Agent Jake Long; and the more she learned the more she was able to gauge his moods.

"I find the whole process interesting. I figured the more I know about the procedures, the better, right?"

"Well yeah, but it's not something you necessarily need to know, as long as I'm with you. I follow the letter of the law."

She gave him a sideways glance and wrinkled her nose at his faux-paux. "Do you?"

He looked at her, eyebrows up to his forehead, almost insulted by her question. "Of course I do. How could you even ask that?"

"I don't mean it as an insult, I'm just saying...I help you with cases in a not so lawful way. Is what I do considered part of that whole letter of the law thing?" Eva looked a little smugly at him, knowing she was pushing his buttons.

He cleared his throat, giving himself a few extra seconds to find the right words to use that would make what came out of his mouth somewhat official. "You have to understand, the police and FBI have been known to use psychics and people like that to help on horrible cases, especially kidnapping cases. We still go by the letter of the law though."

"Okay, I just wondered. Honestly, I didn't mean to upset you. I'm curious as to what comes next if facial recognition doesn't come up with names. What's next?"

Jake slumped in his seat and gave her a palms up. "I don't know yet."

Chapter Thirty

Bright headlights mirrored off of Diego Martinez's office window, making him aware of the visitor. He rounded his desk and walked the length of the hallway that led to the foyer. No sooner did he reach for the door handle, did the bell ring. He opened it to his two men, Miguel and Juan.

"Gentlemen, please come in. To what do I owe the pleasure of this visit?" He motioned them back toward his office.

"Jefe, we may have a problem," Miguel started.

Continuing toward his office, Diego held a finger to his lips, "let's talk about it in my office then."

Knowing that his wife and kids were more than likely roaming the mansion, neither man said another word, until they reached his office, and he shut the door.

Diego stepped behind the bar that stood off on the right wall of his generously sized office, while both men took a seat on the couch. Motioning to the bottles of alcohol lining the back bar, he asked if either one wanted to share in a cocktail with him, but both declined, giving off their anxious vibes.

"So what is the problem? I saw on the news that the woman was taken care of, and in a rather disturbing way, I might add. Where did the two of you come up with that method of disposal?"

He didn't seem the least bit angry with the way Marcella was dealt with, but both men were looking at each other like there was more to it than what he read in the papers. "Boys, what is it, you've got me on pins and needles."

Miguel nodded at his partner, letting him know it was time to speak.

"The thing is, we didn't do that. We dosed their drinks at the bar and when they went to leave, we followed them out. They barely made it to the car, so Miguel put them in Brighton's SUV and I followed them back to his house. Once we got there, we loaded them both onto Alec's boat, and we had already made arrangements for another boat to meet us out there, so we could get a ride back to shore. After we got far enough out, we threw her over the side, figuring she would just drown, then we left the boat there in the middle of nowhere, with Alec passed out. We hitched a ride on our buddies boat back to Brighton's dock, and headed home from there.

We have no idea what happened from there. If anyone saw us on the street with them that night and can identify us, we're screwed."

Diego pondered the new dilemma, and steepled his fingers in front of him, letting out a breath. "So, there was someone else out there that night and pulled her out of the lake, gave her an acid bath, and then dumped her back into the lake, does that cover it?"

Both men nodded.

"And neither of you think Alec could have come to, and finished her on his own?"

"Not even a little. I put twice the normal amount of rohypnol into both of their glasses, and they downed those drinks like they were water," Miguel pointed out.

"And these buddies of yours, they wouldn't be behind this either? You're sure of that?"

"They were both heading down to the Keys on a deep sea fishing excursion the next morning. The timing wouldn't have matched up. And I know they got there, from the photos they posted to social media," Jose stated, very matter of fact.

"So it would seem we have an unknown bee in the hive then," he said as he took out a vial of powder, and a straight razor.

Both men stayed quiet while they watched their leader cut and scrape the powder into an inch long line, then repeat the process until he was satisfied with the texture, and began to snort the line in one inhale.

Diego wiped the excess off of his nose and stood to round his desk, then began pacing back and forth, making the men more and more nervous. Finally, he stopped in mid stride. "Alright, I'm going to put some feelers out and see if some other affiliation is trying to take over my area of the South. You two go about your daily business, and if either of you hear anything out of the ordinary, report back to me, immediately."

Miguel and Juan both knew that was their dismissal and stood up to leave, but Diego stopped them before they made it to the door. "Be careful, we may have a mole in our organization, and if that's the case, dissolving that woman in acid will look like a trip to the spa compared to what I am prepared to do to this person." And with that, he waved them off.

Chapter Thirty-One

Jake was in his room on the first floor, when his phone rang. Noting the number, he immediately picked it up.

"Jess, tell me the good news."

"Well hello to you too, Jake."

"Sorry, hi. How is it going up there?"

"That's better, and it's all good here. I have some good news for you... and some not so good news. Which would you like first?"

He swore under his breath and put a hand to his head to rub the stress headache coming on. "Just tell me everything."

"Okay. The good news is, we identified both men in the video you sent. The taller one is Miguel Romero. He has no priors, he was born in the US, no college education, his work history is spotty, but does work, or at least he did work for Diego Martinez, as a driver the last anyone heard. We were able to get an address from the DMV, which shows he lives in the Buckhead area, at The Hanover Apartment complex. It's pretty high end."

Jake interrupted her as she was about to tell him the second guy's name. "Wait Jess. Did you say he works for Diego Martinez? The big Southern drug kingpin?"

"The one and only."

"I didn't know he relocated to Georgia. Last I heard he was living in South Beach. This just gets better and better. Who's the other guy?"

"Bachelor number two is Juan Perez. Again, he has no priors, but he was born in Tucson, Arizona, a high school drop-out, his work history only has one place on it, and that is his family's restaurant, La Paz, which is in Tucson. We couldn't find a current address for him, especially if he's living in the Atlanta area. He doesn't have a Driver's license issued to him in Arizona or Georgia."

"Great, so what could be the not so good news?"

"Neither of them were a match to the DNA we're looking for. Both men are in their late twenties, so they would only have been six or seven at the time of the first murder.

I emailed you a copy of everything I just gave you, along with a picture of Miguel's license."

Jake let out an expletive that would make your grandmother cringe.

"Sorry Jake. Go pick up the two yahoo's and grill them about who else they're working with or for, and see if presenting them with twenty years in the pen for the drug act will make them talk."

"Yeah, I guess that's all I have to go on. Thanks for all your help Jess, I appreciate it."

"You'll get them Jake, I know you will. Are you using Samantha on this one, or going old school?"

"Samantha? I don't know anyone named Samantha that works with the Bureau."

He heard laughing on the other end, not sure what part of the joke he missed, but once Jess finished her laughing, she let him in on the reason for laughing,

"Samantha Stephens...does that ring any bells?"

No response.

"From the show Bewitched?"

Jake shook his head. He knew a few people were privy to Eva's existence, but didn't realize it was becoming a joke.

"Eva is here with me, and for future reference, don't refer to her that way, okay?"

"Sorry, I didn't mean any disrespect. How's she doing with this case?"

"She's holding her own. Anyway, I gotta check the email and check out the address you sent for Miguel. I'm hoping to get this thing closed in the next day or two. Later Jess."

He'd just pushed the end call button, when he heard a slight movement outside his room.

"Eva, are you out there?" He already knew the answer, but waited for her to show herself.

She walked a couple steps to the doorway and lips turned in, she gave him a sheepish look. She got caught eavesdropping and knew it.

"Hello."

"How much did you hear?"

"Not much really, but I am interested in what your friend Jess called me."

"Of course you heard that. It's nothing really, just let it go."

"Why won't you tell me? I have a bigger back bone than that, Jake. Please tell me. It's not going to break me, I promise."

Jake dropped his head in resignation. "I wasn't even sure who she was talking about at first, but she asked me if I'd brought Samantha in on this case, as in Samantha Stephens from..."

"Bewitched, I've seen it. I guess it could've been worse, she could've called me Winifred Sanford."

"Who is that," Jake asked.

"She's the old ugly witch from the movie "Hocus Pocus." You've probably never heard of it, it's from the 90s."

"No, I have heard of that movie, but I've not seen it."

"What did you find out? I gathered she had news to share with you."

"Yeah, they were able to identify the two guys from the bar. I have to forward this email to Wade and his Dad, and have them pick these guys up. At least one of them. We don't have an address for the second guy."

"After they pick them up, then what?"

"Then I'll go down to the station and question them. And I think I want you there when I do. You were able to get things from Brighton's head, maybe you can do it with these guys, too."

"Okay. I'll leave you to it then," she said, slowly walking out the door.

"Eva," he called after her.

She turned around to see Jake standing in front of her. He didn't say anything right away, so she prodded him to say what he needed to say, then she was going to go to her room.

He pulled her into a hug, and just held her for a minute before speaking. "I'm sorry Jess called you that. I told her it was wrong and not to do it again."

Eva's eyes were closed and her arms were wrapped around Jake's waist. She didn't want to look at him, not yet. She had to gather all of her control, so the tears that threatened to fall, didn't.

She cleared her throat and pulled back from the hug, and looked up at him, "it's nothing I haven't heard before; it's not even the worst name I've been called. The woman from Bewitched is a mom and wife like me, and she's kind, with an extra special talent under her belt."

Jake gave her a full on smile, and let her go wherever it was she was heading to.

Before she could walk too far away from him, he told her, "as soon as we get confirmation from Atlanta PD, we'll head down there, okay?"

"I'll be ready," she said, as she continued down the hallway.

Chapter Thirty-two

Police Chief Holt Montgomery was sitting at his desk when he got a message from Jake to check his email.

Swiveling his chair around to face his computer, he opened the attachment and saw the information that Jake's geek squad was able to get, and blew out a whistle from his lips. "Well well, look what we have here."

He called Wade and made him apprised of the situation, then he called in SWAT to help with the apprehension.

A text message popped up from Jake. "Let me know ASAP when, and if you apprehend the men."

"Smartass..."

His response to Jake was, "what is this "if" crap?"

Wade stuck his head around the corner, all geared up and ready to go. "Are you coming, or staying here?"

"Nah, this one is yours. Be careful."

"Always, Dad."

With his son off to pick up at least one of the suspects, Chief Montgomery returned to his computer and looked into the N-DEX system (National Data Exchange), for any information he could find on Diego Martinez. He wanted to know where family members were, any known associates, and any previous and current addresses he could find on the man. If Diego was indeed in his state and doing business, he wanted to shut it down as fast as humanly possible.

Holt knew of Diego Martinez, he knew him as being one the biggest Drug Kingpins in the South, but the last he heard, the man was still operating out of the Miami area.

Knowing that he may be in his city, gave the chief a migraine.

After typing some basic information into the search bar, four pages of data on Martinez materialized. As he scrolled through a page and a half, addresses were listed. "Oh man, how did I not know he had a house here in the Buckhead area?"

Looking into his arrest record, seemed to bring a whole book of charges that somehow never stuck. It seemed he was always able to get out of it, on technicalities. "Shocker," he said, under his breath. "I wonder how many judges, lawyers and even cops he's got under his nail?"

He emailed a copy of Diego's file over to Jake, in case he needed it, though he figured Jake could probably get even more information on him than he could, with the perks the FBI has.

Holt looked at his watch and noticed that he had been on the database system for over an hour, reading through all the different arrests that Diego Martinez had under him, and he continued to wait on word from the team on whether or not they found Miguel, when his cell rang.

"Chief Montgomery."

"Sir, we were able to apprehend Miguel Romero and Juan Perez. They were both living in the same apartment."

"Were there any issues?"

"Nothing we couldn't handle. Mr. Perez went to bolt for the back bedroom, and Wade took him to the ground. Mr. Romero had his Glock in another room, so he wasn't armed at the time of apprehension."

"Good work. Are you all on your way back to the station? I need to call Special Agent Long."

"Yes sir, we are en route, now."

"Perfect, I'll see you when you get here."

Once he hung up, he immediately sent a message to Jake letting him know they had both of the men in custody, and that they were on their way back to the station.

Not even a minute passed and Jake texted, "On my way!"

Chapter Thirty-three

Eva sat in the brown leather club chair in the corner of their bedroom, reading a book when Jake knocked on the door jamb, "hey, we gotta roll. They picked up our two guys, and they're on their way back to the station."

She placed a bookmark inside the page she was reading and put the book on the nightstand next to her side of the bed, then picked up her shoes and followed him down the stairs.

"Are you sure you need me for this one?" Eva was feeling uneasy about going in with him. She didn't know why, but it was a sick feeling in her stomach. Her gut was rarely ever wrong.

Jake glanced back at her, "I really would like you to be there. If you were able to hear Alec Brighton's thoughts, you may be able to hear these guys. At least that is what I'm hoping for, in case they clam up and refuse to talk."

She nodded briefly, and grabbed her purse.

He noticed her reluctance, which wasn't her normal, "is everything okay?"

"Yeah, fine."

"Eva, tell me. I can see your hesitation and I'm concerned."

She smiled at him, trying her best to hide her undefined fear. "Really, I'm good. Let's go and get this over with."

"No. That's it right there. You never say things like that, at least not since I've known you, granted it hasn't been very long, but I like to think that I can read people pretty good, and you're flowing with angst. And frankly it's making me uncomfortable."

He walked over to where she stood, looked her straight in the eyes; okay, so he had to bend down to do it, but he took one look and saw her fear.

"It's just a gut feeling, that's all. I'm probably just nervous, I'm sure it'll pass."

"Okay, but I'm a big believer in trusting your gut instincts. I promise I won't let anything bad happen to you. They won't even know you're there. You'll stay behind the glass in a room with Chief Montgomery while I question them. I merely want you to see if you can catch onto any of their thoughts."

"Okay, I can do that."

"Good, let's go. It's mid-day, so traffic shouldn't be too horrible."

After they buckled themselves into their seats, Eva's cell rang.

"It's Kris. Do you mind if I answer this?"

"No, go ahead. And let him know we're on our way to the station."

"Hey Kris."

"Hey Beautiful, how's everything going?"

"Pretty good. We just got into the car when you called. We are on our way to the Police station. They picked up two suspects that Jake is going to question. They're the ones that drugged Marcella and Alec."

There was a brief moment of silence.

"Kris? Are you still there?"

"Yeah, I'm here. Um, do you really need to go with him for this?"

She closed her eyes. Eva knew he was worried about her, but like Jake said, she would be behind the glass and no one would see her, and wouldn't even know she was there, for that matter. "I'm going to be behind the glass in another room, watching. Jake's hoping that if the guys decide not to talk, I'll be able to pull something out of their thoughts that he can use."

"Okay, just be careful. And tell Jake, if anything happens to you, I will take it out on him."

"I'm pretty sure he already knows that, but I'll remind him," she replied, with a smile in her voice. "How's your day been? Do you like the office here, in Georgia?"

"It's a nicer office than the one in Ohio, that's for sure. It's newer, too. And the director of engineering inquired whether I'd ever want to move to this office?

Do you think you and the kids could handle the Georgia heat?"

"Seriously, they want you to work at this office full-time?"

"It's a definite possibility, if you'd be on board."

"As long as we don't have to live anywhere near the city. The traffic in Atlanta is gonzo."

A smile lit her face up when she heard Kris laughing on the other end. "Don't worry, I wouldn't want to live close to the city either."

"We agree on that then. If that's what you want to do, I'm game. I certainly wouldn't miss the snow."

"Agreed. But we can talk about it later. You two be safe, and I'll see you later. I have a meeting to get to in a couple of minutes. Love you."

"Love you, too...always and forever."

"Always and forever."

Jake couldn't keep from asking her, "are you guys considering actually moving here? Did I hear that correctly?"

"I guess it's a definite possibility. The director of engineering mentioned it to him. Who knows, we could soon become Georgians. Or would I be a Georgia Peach?" Laughing at her own words, he laughed with her. "I think you'd all be Georgians."

They were turning into the Atlanta Police Department's parking lot, when Jake got the text that they would need to go to the second floor's Homicide Division conference room, before going into the interrogation room.

Once they entered the building, they went through the security checkpoint, collected their belongings from the conveyor belt, headed to the elevator, and up to the second floor. Jake knew this building by heart. He found the conference room where Wade and Holt Montgomery were both seated at the long table, with folders in front of them, waiting.

"Gentlemen." Shaking each of their hands, Jake pointed to Eva, "you both remember my partner Eva St. Claire."

She walked toward them and shook both of their hands. "It's nice to see you, again."

"Are both men in the same room or in separate ones?" Jake didn't beat around the bush, he was ready to get this party started.

Chief Montgomery spoke first, "they're in separate ones, but the room that she can go into will be in the middle of the two rooms. Eva will be able to watch both from the one room. There's privacy glass on both walls, it's a new addition they had put in a few years ago."

"Nice. That will be perfect. Are we ready, or was there something else, first?

"No, we were waiting in here until you arrived. No one has been in there to talk to them yet. If you're ready, we can get started."

"Let's get in there before they completely shut down."

Chapter Thirty-four

Jake walked Eva into a small, unremarkable room that had a table with two uncomfortable looking plastic chairs. On the table she noticed a pad of paper, pen and a bottle of water. Apparently they knew she was coming with Jake.

There was a window on each side of the room that looked into the two separate interrogation rooms.

She looked into one of the windows, where a tall Hispanic man with long jet black hair that had been tied back at the nape of his neck, was sitting. He had a pair of shiny silver handcuffs on and looked quite smug. Eva wondered if the man knew how much trouble he was actually in.

Eva walked to the opposite window and took a quick peek. The man sitting at the metal table had a buzzed haircut, a goatee, and his face was pockmarked from acne that he no doubt suffered from when he'd been a teen. He was dressed neatly, with his dark dress pants, gray dress shirt, black tie and had a single diamond stud in his left ear. What caught Eva's attention was the tattoos that showed on the exposed part of his arms. He had the sleeves of his dress shirt rolled up to right before his elbows, and each arm was adorned with a sleeve of tattoos, some of which looked to be rather intricate in design. She wondered if any of them had a special meaning to them, or if they were possibly gang related. Eva herself had a few tattoos, but each one of hers was carefully selected and had significant meaning.

She heard a door shut on the opposite side of the room, so she made her way over to that window. Jake sat opposite of the bigger man, but he didn't look nervous at all. She assumed this process was old hand for Jake. Eva was sure he had questioned hundreds of criminals before, and this was nothing new. He sat with quiet confidence as he opened a file that he took in with him.

Jake passed an enlarged photo across the table to Miguel. The man looked at it briefly and slid it back towards him.

"Do you recognize the location of this picture," Jake asked.

"No, but I bet you're going to tell me, aren't you?"

"How about if I show you the whole video. That should ring a few bells, I bet."

Jake pulled his laptop open and went to the video feed from the bar where the two suspects are leaning up against the bar, watching for anyone looking while they dropped the contents of the vials into the two drinks that Haven took to Marcella and Alec.

He turned the laptop around and pushed play. "Let me know if anything looks familiar."

Miguel watched the screen for a few minutes, showing zero reaction.

Eva looked on as the man watched the video play out. He showed zero emotion on the outside, but on the inside, now that was a whole different picture. She heard every curse word, fear and anger that the man was projecting. And one in particular stood out from all the others...He didn't kill Marcella.

She knocked on the window to get Jake's attention, and hoped that she didn't upset him by doing that.

Jake heard the knock on the window, and grabbed the laptop, stood up and left the room.

He opened the door, and saw Eva writing stuff down on a tablet, quickly. "What's up?"

Eva looked up, "he didn't kill her."

Looking gobsmacked, Jake gave her a sideways glance, "how do you know?"

She looked at him and smiled that sweet, but wicked smile. She managed to get a sly smile back from him. "Never mind, I think I know how you figured that out. Was there anything else you happened to get off of him?"

"Besides a slew of curse words, there's a lot going on in his head. He's furious, scared and do you know anyone named Diego?"

Jake's eyebrows shot up, "what about him?"

"Apparently the three of them, Diego, Miguel and our other guest over there are on the lookout for who actually killed Marcella. Diego is thinking there's a mole in his organization."

"Crap! Well, I still have these two on drugging charges, so I am still going to see what I can get out of them. This should be fun. I'm going to have Wade and his team pick up Mr. Diego Martinez, he's actually the South's major drug kingpin. That should go over well."

"I'm sorry Jake, but that's what I got out of his thoughts."

"Don't apologize Eva, this is why I need you so badly. You are absolutely invaluable to me."

Eva smiled to herself after he shut the door to go question Juan. A sudden burst of pride welled up inside her. This is why she was doing this, she thought.

*****   *****

Jake walked into the interrogation room where Juan Perez sat, not moving; his head down on the metal table. He laid his laptop on the table, with a thud and Juan flinched. "You are awake?"

"I am now," Juan said. "Was it necessary to slam your computer onto the table?"

"Maybe I was just making sure you weren't sleeping in here. Most guilty people fall asleep to escape the stress of what their body is going through, and it makes them feel like it will all just go away. Frankly, I never understood that myself."

"As you can see, I wasn't sleeping, so I guess that means I don't have a guilty conscience, huh?"

"Oh I don't know about that. Let's see how you answer my questions, first."

Eva had been watching and listening to the back and forth conversation between Jake and Juan. He might talk a big game, but inside this man is a basket case.

"Mr. Perez, do you know Marcella Gallo? She worked for Alec Brighton at Atlantic Sea,Inc."

"Nope, can't say I recognize that name, why?"

"Let me show you a neat little movie here, then." Jake opened his laptop once again, pulled up the file from the bar and turned the laptop around so Juan could see the screen, as he pushed the play button."

Jake watched Juan's face for any signs of guilt. The young man stayed stone faced. Once the video feed finished, Jake swiveled the laptop around and asked Juan, "are you sure you don't want to change your answer on that question I asked, because it looks to me like you and your buddy dosed drinks that specifically went to Marcella Gallo and Alec Brighton."

"So what of it? I gave them a little rohypnol, maybe they needed to lighten up a bit. They looked like they were arguing. I helped them out, amigo."

"You helped them to their car and took them on a boat ride as well, too, didn't you?"

That statement was the first one to make Perez sit up straighter, and Jake noticed that his perfect facade started to fade.

"I have no idea what you're talking about. I've never taken a boat out before."

"Juan, I happen to know you did. Maybe we should talk to Diego, what do you think?"

"What?"

"Diego Martinez... You know, your boss."

"No, don't call him. I'll tell you what I know."

Jake nodded toward the young man to spill it.

"I will plead guilty to the drug charge, but I didn't kill her and neither did Miguel, nor Diego. We took them out on Alec's boat after we left the bar, but all we did was push Marcella over the side. We thought she'd drown, but when she was found completely skinned and dead, we knew someone else had to have been out there that night, and got her out of the lake. They killed her. We left Alec on the boat, passed out. Our friends were waiting to give us a ride back to shore. That's everything I know."

"So you meant for her to die that night though, is that right? Why did you want her dead, to begin with?"

"I didn't kill her. None of us killed her," he kept reiterating.

Eva sat there, deciphering the man's thoughts. She caught onto one thought that may be of interest, and knocked on the window for Jake's attention.

"Juan, think about how you want this to end, okay. I'll be right back."

Jake entered the room, "let me guess, you got something off of Juan that he's not divulging to me."

"I think so. They did want Marcella out of the picture permanently, but like I said, they didn't do it. The reason behind them wanting her out of the way has to do with Diego Martinez using Alec Brighton's boats that are going over to South America. The steering columns are loaded with meth and Marcella caught onto it and threatened to go to the cops if Alec didn't do something about it."

Jake's eyes went wide, "you got all of that from his head, just now? I mean we saw the pictures that Marcella sent her friend, so we knew Alec and his boats had something to do with it."

"It was like the floodgates opened and his head was clogged with information. He may be a cool cucumber on the outer shell, but there's a young man completely freaked out on the inside. They both are."

"Okay, the drug angle doesn't surprise me, really, but the delivery is pretty ingenious. Instead of using people as mules, he's using modes of transportation. That's not a new concept, because I have seen many car air filters filled with bricks of cocaine before. The boats being exported to South America are new to me.

As for the men being scared; it's not me they're afraid of. My money is on Diego Martinez. That man has a catalog full of arrests, but no convictions. I'm sure he has people on the inside that are in his pocket. If he had Police, lawyers, judges and even border patrol on his payroll, it wouldn't surprise me.

I want to know the exact location they left that boat that night, because we need to search the area."

"For what? What do you think you'll find out on the lake?"

With one eyebrow raised, Jake tipped his mouth into a slight grin. "It's what you will hopefully find. Have you ever gone snorkeling or scuba diving?"

Panic was sinking in. Eva cleared her throat and jumped to her feet. "W..wh..why? Why do I need to go into the water?"

"We need to know who pulled Marcella out of that lake that night, Eva. You're the only one who might be able to figure that out, in your own little way. Are there spells for underwater?"

"I have no idea, I'll have to look. Will you be there with me?"

"Of course. I wouldn't let you do this alone."

"Are we almost done here?" Eva's heart started beating in double time.

"Soon. The guys here have enough to hold these guys on drug charges, so they won't be going anywhere, anytime soon. And the sooner we get out on the lake, the better. We have to see if you can find a way to do a water spell. In the meantime, I have to give Alec a call and see if he can take us out on his boat to the exact location he woke up at.

Just hang tight here, and I'll go make the call, and then we'll head back to the cabin. I'll see what equipment we need for the dive, and you can see if you can find a spell that holds up in water."

"Okay."

Chapter Thirty-five

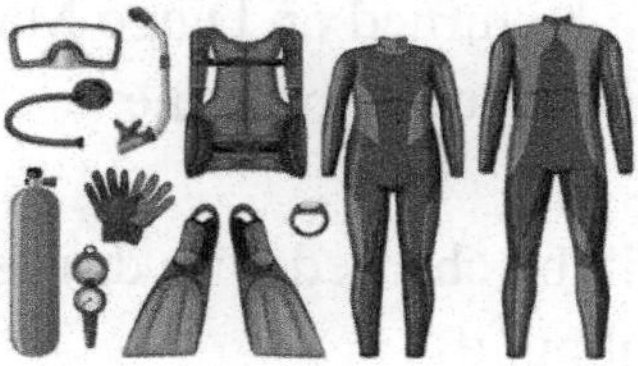

An hour later, Eva and Jake were pulling into Dive at Sea, a scuba diving equipment rental company in Atlanta.

"What do we need to get from here? Do you have a list," Eva asked, feeling uneasy.

"I called them before we left the station and gave them a list of items we needed, so they could have them ready for us. I hope we can go in there, pay for them, and be on our way.

Chief Montgomery is getting a hold of Alec Brighton and arranging for us to meet him at his house, so he can take us out on his boat to the location he was at when he woke up from his drug induced slumber."

"He knows that we know about that?"

"I spoke to him earlier yesterday about it, to see if he would offer up any other information, but he locked up. No doubt, the thought of what might happen to him if he turned on Diego Martinez outweighed the benefits of helping me."

"Won't he still be charged with drug smuggling, since he knew about it?"

"Oh yeah, he will. But, he's thinking if he rats out Diego, he will be a dead man, sitting in prison. Inmates don't take kindly to narcs. If he keeps his mouth shut, he has a fighting chance on the inside," Jake stated, matter of factly.

"That's scary."

"Yeah, and all he cares about is saving his own behind, right now. The only reason he'd be willing to help us with the location in the lake, is because it might help clear Diego; and for Alec, he needs Diego to show him mercy."

"I don't know how he could have gotten into the whole mess with that guy in the first place, when he already had a successful business. Why take such a huge risk?"

"When you have people like Alec, greed is second nature. They are never happy with what they have, they need more. For some reason, it's just never enough for them, and Diego played on that."

Jake held the door for Eva as they entered the store. A gentleman at the front counter asked, "how can I help y'all?"

Jake pulled his badge out, "I called about an hour ago and requested two full sets of diving gear. It's under the name, Jake Long."

The man stood up straighter, "of course, I'm Gary, I'm the one you spoke to. I believe everything is ready to go, I just need a signature on a few forms, from both of you. Liability and all of that."

"We understand. How long do we have before all of this is due back?"

"You have two full days, from the time you leave here. If you need more time, give us a call, and we can renew the rental contract for another two days."

"Two days will be plenty. Thank you."

The man asked Jake, "Do you mind me asking, is this for personal or professional use?"

"A bit of both, actually." Jake hoped that his response placated the man. He wasn't going to go into any specifics with him, that was for sure.

Eva finished signing her forms and passed them back to the man at the counter with a polite smile.

"Okay, I believe all of your equipment is ready to go, so I'll have Justin load it on a cart and bring it out to your car. Normally we ask that everyone who rents our equipment show their certification, but after getting a call from Chief Holt Montgomery, we are respecting his wishes to negate that rule, this time.

Both of you be careful out on the lake, and don't put too much space between you. Always be aware of where each other is. I'm sure you're aware of the rumors that plague Lake Lanier."

"I've read quite a bit about its history, yes," Eva answered.

"Good. Be safe, and we'll see you both back here in two days."

They both thanked the man and made their way back out to the car, where a young man, they assumed was Justin, stood with a cart full of diving equipment.

"Is this all going to fit in the trunk?" Eva wasn't so sure.

Jake smiled back at her, "let's hope."

He opened the trunk and Eva looked in and was surprised at the amount of room it actually had. Both men were able to store all of their gear with room left over.

Justin shook Jake's hand and headed back into the store with his cart. Jake looked over the roof of the car at Eva, "piece of cake."

"The size of the trunk is deceiving from the outside. Admit it, you weren't sure all of that stuff would fit, before you opened it."

"I might have been a little concerned. But if it didn't all fit, I would have put the rest into the back seat."

Chapter Thirty-six

They made it back to the cabin just as Kris was exiting his car. He waved at them with a big smile.

"Kris must have just gotten here, too. I wonder how his day was? I'm hoping it was much more boring than ours was." She rolled her eyes at Jake, showing him she was over it already.

"Yeah, and ours isn't even over yet." He cocked his head at her and gave her a flash of brilliant white teeth.

"That smile of yours doesn't fool me, Jake Long. I know we haven't seen the worst yet, I can feel it," she challenged him. As soon as she said it she cursed herself for letting that statement come out.

His eyebrows pulled together, trying to gauge the truthfulness of that statement. "Do you know something I don't?"

Crap on a cracker! Her inner voice was chiding her for her big mouth.

"No, you know me, I'm a bit of a glass half empty type. I'm always waiting for the other shoe to drop."

"Uh huh." Jake didn't buy it. She knew something, and she wasn't divulging what it was. Before he could confront her on it, her door was opened.

"Hey beautiful! I'm glad to see you back in one piece."

Kris took her hand and helped her out of the car like the true gentleman he is.

She gave him a quick peck on the lips and wrapped her arms around his waist in a big hug. "Why wouldn't I be in one piece," she asked into his chest.

"I wasn't sure what you two were going to get into today, so I'm happy to see that it looked pretty uneventful, that's all."

"Dude, your confidence in me to keep your wife from harm, is truly underwhelming."

Jake gave him a slight punch to the arm, on his way up the steps to the front door.

"I know you can keep her safe, it's the other people out there I don't trust."

Eva unhooked her arms from his waist and grabbed his hand, pulling him toward the steps. "Come on, let's go in. I need to do some research before we leave again."

"Wait, what? Are you guys not finished for today?"

"Nope, I get to go out on a boat with a narcissistic man who may or may not be in cahoots with a very bad drug lord."

The horror on Kris' face made Eva shrink back, "sorry, it's really not that bad."

"I think I'll get the information from Jake, thanks. You go upstairs and do what you need to do," he said, walking away from her.

Her head fell to her chest, and she let out a sigh, "you never learn, do you Eva," she said to herself.

Knowing full well that moping wasn't going to do her any good, she trudged up the stairs to their room and pulled out her book of spells. While she wasn't sure if there was such a thing as a spell she could do under water, she leafed through the pages until she came upon a promising lead.

Eva read through the whole spell and made a mental note of ingredients she would need to take, in order to perform it. She was relieved that she had everything it called for, but in order to complete it correctly, she was going to need Jake. Adding a person to a spell isn't normal and Eva has never done one like this.

*****   *****

Kris followed Jake into the kitchen, "Jake, we need to talk."

He looked over his shoulder, and saw the unease in Kris' eyes. "What about?"

"Eva said you guys weren't done for the evening, and she told me in her own way that you both were going to be going out onto the lake with, how did she put it, "a narcissistic man who is in cahoots with a very bad drug lord."

Jake stifled a laugh that started bubbling up inside him. "She said that?"

"Yes. Now what exactly are the two of you doing tonight? Don't lie to me either."

Letting out a huff, Jake sat on one of the bar stools, "sit, and I'll go over everything with you."

Kris went to the refrigerator for a beer, before sitting down. "I'd offer you one, but I want you completely sober when you are out with my wife."

Sarcasm was in full force with Kris' words and Jake understood the man's attitude and concerns. He had his own list of concerns, but he wasn't about to tell him.

"Eva and I are going over to Alec Brighton, CEO of Atlantic Sea, Inc.'s home on Lake Lanier. He will be taking us out on the lake to the last location he was at, when he woke up after being drugged the night before with Marcella. Once we arrive at the location, Eva and I will be diving, and she is planning on doing some sort of spell under the water, where Marcella was thrown overboard, only to be pulled out by the real killer.

My hope is that she can get a glimpse at who pulled her out, and we can get a grip on the timeline of Marcella's death and nab the one who did it. Now, Chief of Police, Holt Montgomery, who I've worked with many times, years ago, will be accompanying us, but he will stay on the boat with Alec, making sure he doesn't leave us out there in the water."

Kris sat there and took in everything he heard, and was attempting to reign in his emotions. "Jake, Eva hasn't been diving since we went to Puerto Vallarta, eight years ago. She can't be expected to do this, it's the most ridiculous idea I've ever heard. Can't she do the spell from the boat?"

"If I thought it may work from the boat, I'd have her try, but Marcella being pulled out of the water by the unsub happens when she is already sinking to the bottom of the lake. I don't want to risk her having to perform multiple spells. It's too risky."

Eva had already come down the stairs when she heard Kris raise his voice at Jake, so she silently stopped right before the kitchen entrance to eavesdrop on them. She couldn't believe Jake was telling Kris every single detail of what his plan was. She figured Kris would be hellbent on letting her leave the cabin, now.

"If you are doing this dive, I'm going with you," Kris insisted.

"I can't let you go, man. You are still a civilian that I have already told too much too. I'm sorry."

"Well, then I'm taking Eva back to Ohio, and you can figure this crap out on your own, then."

Eva ran into the kitchen and put a hand to Kris's chest and motioned for Jake to keep his mouth shut, so she could say something. Kris was about to say something when she gave him a look that locked him down.

"Kris, I know you're worried about the whole idea of me helping Jake on these crazy investigations, but I have to do this. I used to think I was cursed with the family I was born into, and the DNA that runs through my body, but if I use what I was given, for the greater good, shouldn't I do that? Where traditional means of detective work fail, I can help them succeed at taking one more evil person off the streets, making it just a little bit safer. I know you would do it in a heartbeat, so why can't I?"

Damn it, he hated it when she made a valid point.

Kris closed his eyes for a second, thinking of the right words to say to her. He knew he was acting like a caveman in his attempt to keep her protected, but all he saw was her, and she was his whole world.

"Eva, you're right and I know you're right, but it doesn't change the fact that this whole thing scares the hell out of me. I will always be protective of you, and there's nothing you can do about it..." She was about to challenge his words, and he put his finger to her lips, "but, I see your point, and the determination in those hazel eyes that I fell in love with so many years ago. So, I will put my faith in you and in Jake to come back safely, and unharmed. I will be crazy with worry the whole time, just so you know." He tried for a smile, but it didn't quite reach his blue eyes.

Wrapping her arms around his waist, she held on to her anchor for dear life for a minute, and then let her arms fall away. She looked him in the eyes, letting all her love show. "I love you, even with your caveman tendencies. Always and forever."

He chuckled, which was her goal, and he placed a sweet kiss on her forehead. He whispered into her hair, "always and forever, my Eva."

"Are we about done with the love fest here, we have work to do," Jake said, trying to break the tension.

"Smartass..." Kris said under his breath.

"I heard that," Jake said as he left the room.

Eva shook her head at them as she pulled herself away from Kris' embrace. "I have to go get ready. Everything will be fine, okay?" She got on her tiptoes and kissed his cheek.

Kris watched her walk off and sent up a silent prayer for God to keep watch over her, and to bring her back to him safely.

Chapter Thirty-seven

Jake and Eva pulled into Alec Brighton's driveway and saw the Atlanta Police Department issued Dodge Challenger already there. Chief Holt Montgomery exited the vehicle just as Jake put his rental in park.

The older man walked to their car and waited for them to get out.

"Hey Holt." The two shook hands quickly and Eva sent him a small wave. "I really appreciate you coming out here. I'm going to be in the water with Eva and I don't want to take a chance on Brighton getting cold feet and leaving us out there."

"No problem. I asked Wade to head down this way from the Port Royale Marina with one of the water cops I know up that way. Those two will be an extra set of security, too."

Jake wasn't sure how he felt about all the added people out there. Not everyone knows what Eva is, and what she is capable of. The thought of more people seeing her in action made his hackles stand on end. "Do you really think that's necessary?"

The Chief eyed him skeptically, "Wade knows the capacity in which Eva works with the FBI. He won't say anything to anyone."

"It's not Wade I'm worried about Holt. Alec and the water cop are the ones I'm not comfortable with. If Alec catches a glimpse at what she is doing, it makes me nervous enough, but I was hoping you would keep him distracted, by asking him questions. The other guy, I guess I'll just tell Wade to do the same. It's almost dusk now, so we'll be in the dark soon, which will help. That's why I wanted to go out now. The fewer people see, the better."

Jake stole a glance over his shoulder at her, and saw the look in her eyes. "I'll be as discreet as possible Jake. We'll be under water, so they won't be able to see what I'm doing; at least that's what I'm counting on."

He turned to fully face her, and Chief Montgomery walked off, leaving them to their discussion.

"I didn't mean for it to come out that way. I know you'll do what you need to do, and with the utmost discretion. I just don't want to expose you (anymore) than necessary."

"I know, and thank you for that," she said, pulling her backpack over her shoulder, and walking to the trunk. "Come on, we need to grab all of this stuff out of here, and get moving."

He followed suit and took as much of the equipment out of the trunk as his arms would hold, and headed for the stone walkway that went down to the dock at the back of Alec Brighton's house. She too, filled her arms with as much as she could carry, and followed after him. Between the two of them, they had everything they needed from the car.

Eva looked beyond Jake and saw the lit dock and the large cabin cruiser parked in the water. She wasn't surprised by the size of the boat, Eva knew the man had money, but she had never been on a boat so big; other than a cruise ship, but this was someone's personal boat. She had been on fishing and water skiing boats, sure, but the monstrosity in front of her looked like a house on water. "Wow, that's some boat," she exclaimed.

"Yeah, a little ostentatious, isn't it?" Jake thought the man had more money than brains, especially with his involvement with Diego Martinez.

Holt was already on the boat speaking with Alec when Jake and Eva got to the dock. "Mr. Brighton, could you help Eva by taking the dive equipment out of her hands?"

Alec stepped off the boat, took Eva's load and climbed back into the boat with the ease of a seasoned boater. The boat rocked back and forth at the motion. Jake handed his stuff over to Holt and climbed up on the step and got himself into the boat then turned to grab Eva's hand to help her in. "Here, take my hand and step onto the first step there."

She did as he said, and even though the boat was still rocking, she made it onto the boat without incident. "Thanks. Now, let's hope I don't get seasick," she said with a light chuckle.

Jake's eyebrows rose slightly and Eva saw the question on his face. "I was kidding Jake. I've been on boats before, they don't make me sick."

He gave her an eye roll that made her shake her head and laugh. "Seriously Jake, you need to chill a little."

"Maybe after this is over."

Alec took the diving equipment inside the living quarters of the boat, and came back out, then proceeded to climb the ladder to the helm, so he could start the boat. Chief Montgomery followed up behind him, while Jake and Eva took a seat on the main level.

Alec steered them away from the dock and within a minute he put the boat into high gear, and they were off. Well, as off as a fifty foot boat could go.

Eva's hair blew all around her face and the spray from the back end of the boat where the rotors were, was going into her eyes. She kept flinging her hair out of her face, so she could see, but it landed right back where it was. Pulling her backpack into her lap she searched for a hair tie. Once she located one at the bottom, she held it up in her hand like she just located some treasure. "Yes! I knew I had one in there," she said aloud.

"That'll help keep the hair out of your face," Jake said.

"Yep, the one problem with having long hair is, it gets in your face when you least expect it. That's why I always have one of these babys on me at all times."

He just smiled back at her. His mind was more on what they were about to attempt. Scenarios always played havoc on him. But those worst case ones are what has kept him alive this long, so he let them play out in his mind as they were skipping across the vast water. He noticed the darker the skies became, the more ominous the lake felt. It unsettled him slightly.

They had been traveling along the dark waters for a half an hour when Eva and Jake both noticed the significant slowing of the boat. They looked at each, "we must be getting close to the location he remembers waking to that morning," Jake told her. "Why don't you go in and get your wetsuit on first, then I'll get ready."

"Okay."

Eva stood and entered the interior of the boat, taking her suit down the few steps to where the bathroom was. She still couldn't get a handle on how large and spacious the boat was. "Jeez, this bathroom is bigger than our master bath at home."

After she finagled her way into the suit, but not without breaking into a sweat, she said "My gosh, these things are not made for women as curvy as I am."

She made her way back out to where Jake sat, "you're up."

"Thanks, I'll be back in a minute. You should probably start preparing what you're going to need to do in the water, so we can start when I get back."

She waved him off with a smile, "okay."

Little did he know, the only thing she needed to prepare was him. The spell she found only called for a person to be with her, to hold her hand as a connection to the present.

She was reading the spell that she copied onto a sheet of paper, memorizing it word for word when Jake came out, all suited up and ready to go. He held two tanks, two masks, two sets of fins and two regulators. Eva jumped up to help him, by grabbing one of everything. He set her tank down in front of her.

"Do you have everything ready, I don't see anything but the piece of paper you were just reading?"

"Yeah, this one didn't require much, which is why I chose it."

"Oh, okay. Let's get suited up then, and we'll be on our way. Are you ready to do this?"

"As ready as I'll ever be." She paused for a breath, figuring she should tell him ahead of time what his role in this was going to be.

"Um... there is one thing I need while performing the spell under water," she said, gauging his facial expressions.

"What is that?"

"You."

He was bent over pulling on his fins when he heard her, "Me? Why do you need me for the spell," he asked hesitantly.

"I need to hold onto your hand while I'm in the spell, to keep a connection to the present, since we're going to be under water."

Shaking his head, he said, "I can do that."

"I'm still going to perform a protection spell here on the boat, and pray it works for the water as well," she said, while she grabbed a candle, her white silk scarf, and table salt out of her bag. She set them on the floor, closed her bag and began making the circle of salt, lit the candle as best she could with the breeze coming off the lake, and pulled her scarf around her shoulders. She held out her hand to Jake, and he took it. "You need to stand inside the salt circle with me, since you will be a part of the whole spell process this time. Are you okay with that?" Eva looked up at him, waiting for his response.

He stepped into the circle without hesitation, showing how much he truly trusted her. She let go of his hand briefly to pull her scarf from her shoulders, then with her one free hand, she wove the scarf around their joined hands, weaving it in and out to show the connection.

Eva closed her eyes, pointed her head to the sky, took three deep breaths, and started the incantation.

Elements of the Sun

Elements of the Day, Elements of the
Water Come this way, Powers of night and
day I summon thee, I call upon thee,
To protect me and he...
So Shall it Be.

Jake couldn't take his eyes off of her the whole time she recited the protection spell, he was utterly entranced.

Once she broke contact and undid the scarf, he shook his head pulling himself back to the here and now. He felt how easy it was to lose focus, and simply listen to her words. That left him feeling a little uneasy, but he shook it off. He looked up to see if Alec or Holt were paying them any attention; he was relieved to see them both looking out in the other direction.

Eva was putting the candle out when she heard the other boat moving into position, so she made quick work of putting the candle, her scarf and the container of salt back into her bag.

She grabbed her pair of fins and mask, then went to work putting the fins on her feet, and put the mask on, but sat it up on her forehead, until they went in the water. Jake held her tank up, so he could put it on her back, but stopped himself, to show her the elastics that were placed around the top of the tank. "I want to show you something before I put this on you. See these elastic bands that have a hard metal piece attached to them?'

"Yeah, I was wondering what those were for, I've never seen that on the tanks I've used before, but it's also been a few years since I've gone diving."

"It's another form of communication for us, while we are underwater." Jake pulled at the elastic band and snapped it back quickly. The noise that came from the movement made a loud pinging noise. "Now under water, that will sound so much different, and it will vibrate the tank, so you will not only hear the vibration, but you'll feel it, too."

"That's pretty cool."

Jake put her tank over her shoulders and let it go gently, because it wasn't light by any means. The air tank carried around 3000 PSI. They can go anywhere from 2000-3500 PSI. He handed her an SPG (Submersible Pressure Gauge) that attaches to her regulator. The one each of them is carrying has a three gauge console, so not only did it give them the amount of gas remaining in their tanks, but it also displays the depth at which they are at all times, and a compass.

Eva looked at the gauge in awe, "what are all of these dials for? I recognize the PSI gauge, but what are the other two?" She read some numbers on the one, and noticed the other had the North, South, East and West indicators on them. "Never mind, I think I know. This one tells me how deep we are and the other is for direction, like a compass."

"Exactly," he said, as he threw his tank over his shoulder with ease.

Jake passed Eva a flashlight to connect to her mask, and her regulator. She plugged her SPG into the regulator, clipped on the flashlight and was ready to go.

"Let's do this," he said.

"Hold on Jake, I wanted to let you know that the only thing I'll need from you in the water while I do the spell is your hand."

"You mean to hold my hand?"

"Yes. I'll recite the spell in my mind and all I need you to do is hold my hand the whole time. You are my connection to the present, since I'm going back in time to that night Marcella was thrown overboard.

I've never done a spell like this, so bare with me, okay? Just don't let my hand go."

"I won't let you go, I promise." And he was dead serious, too. He would put his life on the line to keep her safe.

Holt and Alec looked over the top, down at the pair, and Holt asked Jake, "are you all going in now? Wade and his buddy are over there, west of us about 200 feet."

"Yeah, we are going in."

Eva nodded with a smile, and jumped into the dark water. Jake followed right behind her. Once in, Eva pulled her mask down over her eyes and nose, and turned the light on. She gave Jake the thumbs up, and they dove into the water.

She felt lucky to have the light, because she wouldn't have been able to see her hand in front of her face otherwise. That was good thinking on Jake's part.

They swam until they were at a depth of 125 feet. Eva stopped swimming and turned towards Jake, motioning him to come closer to her. He swam until he was a foot away from her. She gave him the thumbs up, and she hoped that he understood that that meant she was going to start the incantation.

Eva held out her hand and Jake grabbed hold of her and pulled her a little closer. His grip was firm, but it wasn't hurting her.

As she closed her eyes, she formed a picture of a clock and calendar in her mind, just as the spell showed. She knew the date and the time that she needed, or at least an approximate time from what Juan and Miguel told Jake.

Jake's hand was soft around hers, and a sense of calm replaced her anxiety. She gave his hand a little squeeze and opened her eyes to see him somewhat smiling at her. She nodded once and let her eyes close once again, and brought the calendar and clock back into her mind's eye.

Eva began the spell.

*Oh mighty time, I wish to time travel
to the past.
Bring me to the past where Marcella took
her last, then back to the present
So mote it be.*

Eva began to feel a swirling vortex around her. Jake's hand loosened around hers, and she grabbed on tighter as the circular whirlpool began to slow down. She opened her eyes and gave Jake an all is okay sign with her other hand.

*****   *****

Jose Vergara couldn't believe his eyes as he was watching the live feed from his drone that he was maneuvering over the lake.

He saw the water turn into a whirlpool and kept his drone on that spot. He knew Alec Brighton was out there manning his big boat with the cop, and FBI agent, but he didn't yet know who the female was. She went into the water with the fed, but he knew she wasn't a federal agent.

He was curious as to what they were looking for under the water though. They had already found the office manager and as far he was concerned, there was nothing left of her but bones. He made sure of that.

He hoped that Martinez would be grateful to him for cleaning up his mess, yet again. Jose didn't need any problems coming back to him, he had a family both here and in Juarez that Diego consistently held over his head.

Those three idiots couldn't get rid of someone to save their lives.

*****   *****

Eva watched on as Marcella entered the water and began to sink further into the abyss. About thirty seconds in, Marcella's body jerked and started flailing. The flow of water rushing over her after being thrown over the boat must have jolted her conscious.

She looked over at Jake and his eyes were as round as saucers. He was seeing the same thing she was, which meant he was inside the spell with her.

Ignoring his tugs, Eva kept watching the scene fold out in front of her. Marcella was making her way to the surface, so Eva pulled Jake along with her to see what happened from here. Once she made it to the surface, she took in several gasps of air and coughed up water. She began looking around frantically in the darkness for anything resembling help. Marcella saw an outline not far from where she was floating and swam toward it, hoping it might be some fishermen at least. The small craft was moving closer to where she was, and Eva saw a male lean out of the boat and offer her a hand, to which she began to take, until she got a closer look at her savior, then she started pulling away from him. He'd already had a tight grip on her arm and wasn't letting go and with Marcella already being somewhat incoherent from the drugs in her system, she didn't have the strength to get away.

Once the man had her on his boat, he shackled her hands and ankles to a metal bench within the boat, then took off slowly at first. Eva tried to narrow in on any markings that stood out on the boat. That's when she noticed the back end where there was a name and boat number. Eva made a mental note of the name and number. She turned her head to Jake, who saw them as well, and gave his head a small shake.

They both pointed at the same time, when they saw Alec's boat off in the distance. He was on that boat completely unaware of what had happened.

Not sure if they were going to see anything else, Eva decided that this was probably a good time to head back to where they were when she started the spell, so they could get back to the present time. Still holding onto Jake's hand, she pulled him closer to her body and motioned them to dive back down.

Once they made it to the original depth, Eva thought for a second, and held her index finger up to him in a "hold on a second" gesture. Jake nodded to her. Eva decided to push her time travel spell forward two days. That was the timeline that the authorities presumed was the day Marcella was put back into the water to be found.

She knew Jake probably wasn't going to like this, but she had no way of telling him her plan, so she continued doing what she did at the beginning, but adjusted the date.

When the water again started going into a swirling vortex, Jake assumed they were returning to the present time, until she pulled him to the water's surface and floated there for a few seconds, and Jake didn't see the boat they had come out here on, anywhere.

He ripped his regulator out of his mouth and unhooked his hand from hers, "where is Brighton's boat, and the boat Wade was on?"

Eva's eyes went wide, and she took her mouth piece out and yelled, "hold onto my hand, we aren't out of the spell, I pushed the time travel date forward a couple days, to see if the same person who took Marcella is the same person who dumped her bones back into the water."

Jake immediately grabbed for her hand, but came up empty. His hand floated right through hers.

"Oh my God, this isn't good," he said. He saw the terror in her eyes. "Can you hear me, Eva?"

She shook her head yes, and Jake threw up a silent thank you to the man upstairs.

"What happens now?"

"I don't know. I told you I'd never performed this spell before, so this is all new to me. Why did you let me go? You promised you would hold onto me."

The emotions in her voice gutted him on every level. He let her down. "I'm sorry Eva, I thought we were out of the spell when you pulled us to the surface."

She started to respond, but got pulled under in a rapid jerk movement. Jake yelled, "Eva!!"

Eva was being dragged through the water at a fast pace. She brought her hand up to where her regulator was flopping over her shoulder, and attempted to put it back into her mouth, so she wouldn't drown. Once she got it back in, she had to release a few breaths out, because obviously water had gotten inside the tube. She looked down at her ankles and saw a hand on each one. She used every bit of strength she could muster to pull herself away.

Jake pulled his mask down and inserted his regulator within seconds of her disappearing, and dove back under the water. His flashlight was at least helping him maneuver through the dark murky water, but he didn't see her anywhere.

Eva felt the hands tighten around her ankles and it was starting to hurt. She began talking to herself, "Gram help, what am I supposed to do? I'm going to die down here."

She knew she wouldn't actually get an answer, but if she kept talking, it meant she was still alive, right?

"Eva darling, what did I tell you, you are much more powerful than you realize. Now is a good time to see what you can do."

Eva thought she was losing it, did she actually just hear a whisper in her ear that sounded like her grandmother? Was she getting delirious?

"I have more power than I realize..." She let that sink in for a few seconds and decided that this was not the way she was going out.

She closed her eyes, all while careening to the bottom of the lake by the hands of God only knows what, and she found her calming center. She recognized the light in the center of her core, it was the same white light that took on her own mother. The more she focused on that light the bigger it got.

Eva shot her hands down toward her ankles, where the hands carrying her, had her in their grasp, when a bright white light emanated from her fingertips. The force was so strong that the hands unclasped her ankles and Eva looked down and saw a figure floating closer to her. It was human, or it used to be anyway. Eva could see that it was a female entity and by the way it was dressed, she had been dead quite a long time. It took her a minute to figure out, but when it hit her, she was stunned. This was one of the spirits that would drag innocent people to their watery deaths.

The spirit floated up to meet her eyes. They stared at each other briefly and Eva tried to talk to it telepathically. She wasn't sure it would work, but it was worth a shot. The look on the spirit's face was that of confusion, and something else.

"Why did you try to drown me," Eva projected the question to her.

The female spirit's head looked back and forth wondering where the question was coming from. Eva waved and pointed to herself, letting her know that it was indeed her that was talking to her. "This is so weird," Eva thought.

The watery figure dropped her head in shame, and Eva heard what she thought was a southern accent coming through saying, "They left us here in this dark watery grave. My family can't even visit my grave site. All who enter these watery depths should have to live as we do."

"I'm so sorry that they built this lake over your final resting place, that wasn't fair to you or your loved ones. But this was done more than sixty-six years ago, so whoever built this lake has probably long passed on by now, too."

The spirit shook her head in response to Eva's comment and gave her a sad look, then she took off.

Eva didn't know what to think about any of this, she just wanted to get back to where Jake was. She started swimming back up and stopped to take a look at her depth gauge and saw that she had been dragged down over two hundred feet.

A light moving in the water above her caught her eye, and she followed it. When she caught up to it, she saw Jake and swam as fast as she could to him. He tried to wrap his arms around her when she was within reach, to try to get her back to the surface, but his hands continued to go right through her. She motioned for him to swim upward toward the surface. Once they both broke through to the surface, they both removed their regulators. "Jesus Eva, what the hell happened to you? One second you were there and the next you were swept away."

Her breathing was raspy from the intake of water from earlier, so her response came out hoarse. "You're not going to believe it. Remember when I told you that drowning survivors felt like they had hands wrapped around their ankles?"

"Yeah."

"Well, they were right. I came face to face with an old spirit that has been down there a long time. I checked my depth meter before I started back up, and she'd taken me down over two hundred feet."

"You saw her? Did she look human?"

"I saw her, and I was able to get her hands off of my ankles, too. But, I'll save that story for another time. So the rumors are true. This lake is very much haunted."

"Jeez, the more I hang around you, the weirder stuff I experience."

Eva tried a smile, "you act like that's a bad thing."

Jake was about to give her a retort when they both heard a motor coming their way. He held a finger to his lips to keep her from talking. He shut off his flashlight and she did as well. It was pitch black out on the water, not even the sliver of moon that was shown gave them much light to see by.

The surrounding water began to wake, which meant the boat was getting closer.

Eva did her best to focus on the moving silhouette heading in their direction. The motor was turned off and started drifting toward them. Jake moved closer to Eva, in case she needed him, then he remembered he couldn't touch her. Frustration billowed inside him, but he pushed it aside and focused on the boat coming at them. They both swam a few feet away from the oncoming craft, when she saw something being rolled over the edge and then a splash was heard.

Eva quickly put her mouthpiece in and dove under the water to see what was thrown in. Jake swam closer to the boat to get a glimpse of the driver, and the boat itself before it took off. He saw the numbers and the markings, but wasn't surprised to see that they matched the ones they saw previously when Marcella had been pulled out of the water.

Eva followed the skeleton down and knew that it was Marcella, just as she assumed it would be. She hoped Jake had been able to get a look at the driver before they took off. She watched the boney corpse continue its fall to the bottom, when a filmy form appeared over top of it, looking directly at her. It was Marcella. Eva's eye's got big, seeing how the apparition moved with the remains. She swam her way down as fast as she could to see if she could get anything off of her. She had been able to communicate with the other one, why not this one, too.

"Marcella," she projected out of her mind.

The apparition of Marcella's head turned toward Eva. Her eyebrows were scrunched together. She was confused and scared.

Eva continued to follow, and project questions to her, hoping to get something back. "Who did this to you? Do you know?"

Marcella's head nodded yes, and then Eva heard two words come through, "Steering column."

"Steering Column? She thought about it for a second, when she saw Marcella continue to descend farther down to the bottom.   Eva took one look at her SPG console and knew she wouldn't be able to go any farther, because her PSI levels were getting dangerously low.

Eva swam back up to the surface praying that Jake was able to get something substantial off of the boat or the driver.

When she finally broke through the surface, Jake was waiting for her. He had his mask resting on his forehead, and his mouthpiece hanging to the side. He looked over at her, "are you okay?"

She nodded, and began taking her mask off and her mouthpiece out to answer him and to tell him what Marcella said. "I'm fine. I saw Marcella's skeleton descend, and her apparition appeared as it was sinking. It was so surreal. I managed to ask her if she knew who did this to her."

Jake's eyebrows reached the top of his hairline, "and did she give you an answer?"

"All she said was "steering column", do you have any idea what that means?"

Jake thought about it for a minute then remembered that Marcella had taken pictures inside the plant of a man putting the drugs into the steering columns of the boats that were being exported to South America. "It's the guy she took pictures of that she saw inside the plant that night."

"We have to get back to present time and find out who that is," Eva said. "And we have to do it quickly, Jake. My PSI is getting low, how's yours?"

Jake checked his console, and he still had 1500 PSI showing on his, but he wasn't dragged under water a little bit ago either.

"Okay what do we do? We aren't attached to each other anymore, so how's this going to work?"

"You'll just have to trust me, okay? Can you do that?"

"Of course."

"Then put your stuff back on and let's dive back under, where we started."

They both put their gear back on and dove simultaneously into the water. Eva watched her depth meter as she swam downward. When she reached 125 feet, she stopped, as did Jake.

They floated in place while Eva gathered her thoughts on how to get them both back to the present time.

She thought, "Gram, it would be great if you could help me figure this one out."

You know what to do Eva, trust yourself.

"Easy for you to say."

A faint laugh came through, which made Eva roll her eyes.

"Okay, I guess I'm going to have to figure this out on my own." She found her white light faster this time, and it was ebbing and flowing just under the surface, as if it was waiting for her to tell it what to do.

She raised her hands out in front of her, to where Jake floated. He was eyeing her with such hope in his eyes. She could see them through his mask perfectly. The light began moving through her arms, and she focused that light out toward Jake's waiting hand. He jerked slightly, and looked at his hand, which was now glowing with white light. His face was torn between fascination and fear. The contrast made Eva chuckle to herself. "Gotta keep him on his toes."

Eva pulled her hand closer into her body, and noticed as she did this, Jake too, was moving. It took all of ten seconds to mold his hand back into hers, and she felt his soft smooth flesh against her hand, and let out a silent sigh of relief.

She let her eyes close slowly and went to her mind's eye and changed the date and time to the present and started the incantation.

Oh I plead to go back to our own time,
So that we may see our family again,
So mote it be.

She squeezed Jake's hand just a bit tighter as she felt the water swirl around them again. Within seconds the motion ceased, and they both stared at each other for a second. They were still connected at the hand, so she pointed her other finger upward, and they swam to the surface.

As soon as their heads were out of the water, they both ripped off their masks and took out their regulators, taking in breath after breath of fresh air.

She pulled Jake into an awkward hug, considering the bulky gear they were wearing, but she didn't care, she'd gotten them back safely.

"You did good Eva."

Eva smiled back at him, "thanks Jake."

Multiple flashlights pointed down at them. Chief Montgomery yelled, "are you both okay? What the hell happened out there, you've been under the water for over a half an hour."

Jake nodded, "we are both fine." Then he looked at Eva, "did it seem like over thirty minutes to you?"

"No, more like five hours."

He wasn't sure how insulted he should feel about that remark, but he let it slide, they had more important things to worry about now. He knew who killed Marcella, but he didn't have a name.

"Holt, I know who killed Marcella. Ask Brighton there if he has a name of the guy who comes in to fill the boats before they leave."

Even in the dark Jake could see the color drain from Brighton's face.

***** *****

Jose still had the drone fifty feet above them watching and listening to everything they were saying. With both boats engines running, they had no idea he was above them.

He knew something strange was going on, because the flashes of light under the water definitely weren't from the lights attached to their masks. One word came to mind when he thought of the female with the fed. "Bruja."

"Well isn't that something. I haven't seen a Bruja in many years, and that was in Juarez. I wonder if all of them down there know what she is," he said to himself. "That's the only explanation for them knowing it was me. They just didn't have my name yet. You better keep your mouth shut Brighton."

The drone he was using had maybe five to ten minutes left of air time, so he maneuvered it so it was now heading back to where he was camped out, on the other side of the lake. The model he flew was top of the line with infrared night vision capability, which meant it didn't need lights to capture video.

After finding out Diego's boys were arrested, he began following Alec. When he saw the cop and the federal agent show up, and they had diving gear with them, Jose knew exactly where they were headed.

Merely talking to himself, he began forming a plan. "I think I'm going to have to go have a talk with Mr. CEO, and make sure he doesn't reveal my name. Little miss Bruja may have to be dealt with as well."

He heard the rotors from his drone in the distance, as it came in closer. Once he landed it on the rocks, he picked it up and started packing it away, so he could get out of there.

*****   *****

"Start talking Alec. You heard what Agent Long said. ``Who is the guy that comes in to do the packing?"

Alec's face took on a whiter shade and his posture went rigid. "I don't know his name, or if it's even the same guy every time. Martinez has a key to the plant, and when I know it's the day of packing, I leave before they arrive. I swear."

Eva and Jake were back on the boat when Holt descended the ladder. He needed to talk to Jake with her out of ear shot, but he didn't want to be rude, he thought she was a very nice person, but she was still a civilian.

"Chief Montgomery," she acknowledged, as she walked past him, on her way inside the cabin area. "I'm going to change out of this uncomfortable wetsuit, if you'll both excuse me."

Thankful that he didn't have to end up asking her to leave, Holt sat on the bench across from where Jake sat, drying himself off. He cleared his throat and Jake looked up, "what is it?"

"He's saying he doesn't know the name of the guy, he's not even sure it's the same one every time, according to him. And he says he leaves before they even get there."

Jake let out an expletive that would rival a sailor. "Nothing can ever be easy, can it?"

"Sorry Jake. I'm not entirely sure I believe him though. He's probably scared and trying to save his own hind end.

Do you want to take another crack at him?"

"Yeah, once we are back at his house, right now I want to change my clothes, drink some water and think for a few."

"Did you already have the pictures Marcella took of the guy that night, run through facial recognition?"

"I did and they came up with nothing. The closest they got was 60% match. I do have the boat identification name and numbers that were on the side of the boat he used, so I'll run those as soon as we get back to the dock."

"What? How did you find that out, and when?"

Jake gave his old friend a slight smirk before saying, "you probably don't want to know."

It took the man a minute to process what he said, "ah, yeah I don't need to know."

Eva showed up on the other side of the sliding glass door, dressed in her street clothes again. She pulled the door open, as Chief Montgomery began climbing back up to the helm with Alec.

"Is everything okay?"

"Sort of. Alec's not giving us a name yet. I'll talk to him once we get back to his house."

"How could he not know the guy?"

"I think he's scared, to be honest. He saw what they did to Marcella, so what makes him think they won't do the same thing to him."

Eva thought about it, and she could sort of agree with that logic, but also thought that if he gave up the name, the FBI could protect him. This wasn't her rodeo though, so she didn't voice her opinion.

Chapter Thirty-eight

Once they got the boat docked, they sent Wade and his buddy back, then grabbed all their gear, stowed it away in the trunk of their rental and went back into Alec's home.

Eva walked through the door and felt her mouth drop open. She noticed the whole back of the house was a wall of windows. "Wow..."

Jake took in what she was seeing and agreed, wow definitely covered it.

They all sat around the island in the massive kitchen, when Alec said, "there's nothing else I can tell you, I don't know the name of the guy or guys Martinez has come in. I told Chief Montgomery that when we were on the boat."

"You realize you are still going to go to jail on the drug smuggling charge, right? There is no avoiding it. I can't tell if you're scared, because of what might happen to you if you give me a name, or if you're just stupid."

"You'd be scared too if Diego Martinez had a hold over you."

Eva sat up straighter, looking from Jake to Alec and finally asked, "can't the FBI put him in witness protection or something, if he feels his life is in danger? You know, he gives you the evidence, and he gets protected."

"It doesn't always work that way Eva, every case is different. Nothing is set in stone when a defendant turns over evidence against a bigger fish."

The coloring in Alec's face was growing paler by the minute. He wanted them all to leave and Jake felt his discomfort. Unfortunately, it wasn't going to change the fact that he was going to arrest Alec sooner than later.

They had placed a plain clothes officer in the neighborhood where Alec lived, so Jake wasn't too worried about Alec fleeing, so he stood and motioned for Eva to join him.

He walked up to Alec Brighton, stood not even six inches from his face, "think about what you're doing, Mr. Brighton. There is no amount of money that will keep you out of jail."

And with that, Eva and Jake took their leave, with Chief Montgomery trailing behind them.

"Jake, hold up."

The look of pure frustration showed in the older man's features when he caught up to them at their car.

"What?"

"You're just going to let him stay in his palatial home here? You're not arresting him tonight?"

"No, I want to see if I give him some time, he'll come to his senses, and I know one of your guys is sitting nearby, so if he tries to leave, I'll know.

Go home and get some sleep, Holt. That's what I need to do, and I need to get Eva back to the cabin, she's exhausted. I'll have my team run the boat numbers and the name I saw on the side and see where that leads us."

"Okay, this is your show. I'll see you in the morning."

"Holt, this is our show, not just mine. We are all pulling together to figure this out."

Chapter Thirty-nine

Eva woke with a start at something nudging her. It took a minute to focus on the dark. She looked around and found Jake sitting in the driver's seat staring at her and trying to hold back a smile.

"Where are we," she asked around a yawn.

"We're back at the cabin Sleeping Beauty, it's time to get you into an actual bed."

Pulling herself into an upright position, she peeked through the window of the dash and squinted her eyes trying to see the outline of the cabin. "I'm sorry I fell asleep on the ride back. I'm sure I gave you my striking rendition of "Snore River". Heat bloomed in her cheeks as her embarrassment took over.

"Actually, I didn't hear a peep out of you."

"Oh, thank God." Hearing him say that made her feel better.

"Alright sleepyhead, let's get inside and you can tell Kris all about our adventure," he motioned for her to grab her backpack.

"It looks like he's still up, the porch light just went on, or is that motion activated?"

Jake looked up to the front door just as Kris was stepping out. "He's still up and currently en route to probably carry you into the house."

"He couldn't carry me, if he tried. I'd probably break his back, or give him a hernia," she said, slightly amused.

Jake hollered over the top of the car. "Hey Kris, your wife doesn't think you could carry her into the house, do you want to prove her wrong?"

Eva was dumbfounded by his comment and looked back at Kris to see him running toward her, laughing. "Oh Crap," she yelled.

Kris bent down and put his arms around her knees, then proceeded to hoist her over his one shoulder. He walked around the back of the car and headed for the front door. She started laughing so hard, she feared she may pee. "Put me down!"

"I will, once I get you upstairs to your bed."

Eva lifted her head to stare daggers into Jake. It was a completely lost cause, because all she got back was a laugh, and a finger wave.

Kris made it up the stairs and to the end of the hall where their bedroom was, and flopped her onto the bed, then fell face first right next to her. She was still giggling and that sound alone was music to Kris' ears. One of the first things he remembers falling for was her cute laugh. He could listen to that all day, and not get bored.

"So, are you going to tell me how everything went? You're here in one piece, so that's a huge plus."

"It went as I expected. We saw most of what we needed to see, and a few extra things."

"What extra things," he asked cautiously. He rolled onto his side, so he could look at her. "I want to hear everything, so start at the beginning."

She rolled her eyes, "it's not that bad. I will tell you this, I did see one of the so-called spirits of Lake Lanier. I even communicated with her for a brief moment." Eva left the part out about the spirit trying to take her to her own watery grave. He didn't need that mental picture.

"Whoa, really? What did it look like?"

"It was a female, and she looked to have been from the 1920s or 30s, if I had to hazard a guess, by the way she was dressed."

"That's cool. Anything else?"

Eva sat up and moved to the end of the bed, so she could stand and go get ready for bed. "Not really. I'm just glad it went okay. I'm going to go take a quick shower, and then I'm crashing hard."

Kris waved her off. He could see she was dragging and probably exhausted.

Chapter Forty

Jake sat at the dining table and opened his laptop. Pulling up his email, he started to compose an urgent message to his team asking them to check into the boat name and registered number that he pulled off of it last night. He's crossing his fingers that they can get some useful information off of it, that he can use. The numbers he pulled should give them at least the name of who it is registered to, if nothing else.

He was feeling the weight of the day on his shoulders, and exhaustion was beginning to set in. Sleep was next on his list of things to do.

Kris came over to where he was sitting and pulled a stool out and waited until he finished his email. Once he hit send, he closed up his laptop, pushed it aside and walked over to the refrigerator, opened it and grabbed two beers, handing one over to Kris, before shutting it back up.

"I see a lot of questions on your face, what's up?"

"First off, thank you for getting her home safely, and second, did she tell you about the apparition she communicated with under the water?"

"Kris man, your wife is stronger than you think, she can take care of herself, but it won't ever stop me from protecting her when we are out in the field. You can always count on that. And, not only did she tell me about the apparition, I saw first hand how it pulled her under faster than anything I've ever seen in my life."

"Wait, what? It pulled her under? She failed to mention that part."

Jake cursed under his breath. She didn't tell him the whole story, and now he was going to get the brunt of the man's irritation. "Like I said, she is stronger than you think. Eva took care of it. I'm not sure what all she did to get rid of it, but I'll say this, her powers are not limited to just mere spell casting. I saw a beam of light in the water and then felt everything around me shake; kind of like a low level earthquake. She resurfaced thirty seconds later, telling me about it."

"Jesus," Kris exclaimed, grabbing for his beer and taking a long pull. "I have no idea what I'm dealing with here anymore, Jake. I knew within months of dating her, of her past. She didn't keep it from me, but she also told me that she vowed never to go back to that part of her.

What her mother did was beyond wrong, and that alone left a bad taste in my mouth. The only family of hers that I've ever met was her sister. And I've only seen her a handful of times.

But since she has opened this can of worms back up, she's changing. What am I supposed to do or think about this?"

Jake sat quietly, listening to his buddy, and he understood the feelings he was going through, he really did, but none of what Eva has done thus far that he's witnessed, wouldn't change the way he felt about her as a person. Yes, she has some odd gifts, but not once had he seen or felt that any of them were dark or disturbing, in nature, but he wasn't the one married to her, he thought to himself.

"Kris, let me ask you a personal question... What is the first thing that comes to mind when I say unconditional love?"

"Her."

"You see that... that was an immediate response and your true feelings toward her. Whatever it is she is going through right now, isn't important in the grand scheme of things. She is still your Eva, the Eva you fell in love with, and are still in love with. She may just have a few extra special qualities about her. But she is embracing them and using them for the greater good, not for evil. And that, my friend, is what you need to remember."

A smile formed on Kris' face, and he gave his head a small shake, "I hate when you get all philosophical on me."

Jake laughed and clinked his bottle with Kris'. "It's what I do."

Chapter Forty-one

Sun spilled through the partially opened curtains, making Eva roll over to the opposite side to grab her phone to see what time it was. When she saw that it was 11:30am, she whipped the covers off and clambered out of bed and into the bathroom.

"How could I have slept so late, I never sleep past 8:30," she said out loud to herself.

The hot water from the shower flowed down over her achy muscles. Her legs were especially sore from all the swimming she did last night.

She stood under the water, letting the heat soak in, until it ran cold.

Today is going to be a good day, she thought. She wasn't going to have to go into the station with Jake, and Kris was already at the office, so she figured she would take her book, and sit outside in one of the rockers that she'd noticed on the porch.

Dressed, hair blown dry, and put into a ponytail, Eva made her way down stairs and into the kitchen, where she found a pot of hot coffee, already brewed, a large blueberry muffin, which was her favorite, and a note next to it, from Jake. *Good Morning Sleepyhead! I'm giving you a break today and heading into the station to meet Chief Montgomery. If you need anything, call or text me. See ya later, Jake"*

She thought she had heard both men leave earlier, so this wasn't a surprise, but the muffin and coffee were a welcome present.

Looking for a coffee mug, she found the biggest one in the cupboard, grabbed it, and saw a folded piece of paper inside. Unfolding the paper and reading it, a smile bloomed on her face. It was from Kris. *Good morning, beautiful! You were sleeping so peacefully, I didn't want to wake you when I left this morning, so I figured you would be in need of a BIG cup of coffee, after last night, so I stuffed this little note into the biggest one I could find. If you're reading this, do I know you, or what? LOL. Anyway, I hope you get to relax some today, and I'll see you later. Love you, always and forever, Kris*

Eva swiped a stray tear from her cheek and proceeded to pour herself some coffee, then she snagged the muffin, along with a fork and napkin, then headed out to the front porch. Setting her coffee on the porch floor, she proceeded to dig into the muffin. "Oh yum!" Savoring the moist cake and the sweet berries, a sigh came out.

*****   *****

Alec walked out his back door, heading toward his boat to do a little bit of maintenance, when he heard the crunch of rocks near the side of his house. He detoured over to the left side of his house where a Hispanic male was walking toward him.

"Can I help you?" Alec stopped and watched the man continue to close in on him. He started backing away, when the man finally spoke. "Stay right where you are Mr. Brighton," the man said, now holding a gun out towards him.

Alec sucked in a whoosh of air and stood stock still. "What do you want? Money? I can give you that. Do you want my boat? Drugs? I'll give you whatever I have, just don't hurt me.

The man let out a bark of laughter. "You really don't recognize me, do you? And here I was, all worried that you opened your big mouth to the federal agent last night."

Alec took in the obvious Spanish accent and felt shivers run up his back. "You're the one who killed Marcella," he said, as more of a statement than a question.

"You're quick amigo. What did you tell them?"

"Nothing. I told them nothing, because I don't know you or your name."

"Who's the female that is with him, all the time?"

"All I know is that her name is Eva. That's how he introduced her to me. I don't think she's an FBI agent though. Actually, I'm not sure what she is, to be honest. She was doing some weird stuff last night," Alec said, thinking back.

"I know what she is. She's a Bruja and I need you to get her to come over here."

Alec cocked his head, "a what?"

"A Bruja is a witch. And she is a real spell casting witch. You get her over here, and maybe, just maybe, I won't have to kill you."

Confusion set in and Alec didn't know which end was up. A witch, he thought; those things actually exist? Then the real problem hit him, "how am I going to get her here, I don't have her contact information. How do you expect me to do that?"

Jose laughed, "I have the information you need." He held a phone in his other hand, while the gun remained pointed at Alec. "I have some pretty genius friends, and this phone is a clone of that FBI agent's phone, with her number in the contact list and everything. You are going to text her saying that you need her to get a ride over to your house, she'll think she is getting a text from her FBI agent, and she will do as she is asked."

Alec took the phone, and noticed that the screen was already set to the text message app, and her contact information was displayed. He typed in the message and hit send.

*****   *****

Eva was relishing in reading her book, sipping her coffee, and rocking in the rocker on the porch, when her phone dinged, indicating a text message. She pulled her phone out of her pocket and read the message. It was from Jake. "Well crap on a cracker.

How am I going to get over to Alec Brighton's house without a car?" She thought about it for a second, then texted him back. I have no car, how would you like me to get there? Why didn't you just come here before going to his place?

She got a reply that was almost immediate, "grab an Uber, quick."

Eva went to her Uber app and requested a car. She wasn't even sure they would be able to come out this way, but she got confirmation that one was in the area, and would be there momentarily. "Great," she said sarcastically.

She grabbed her book, plate and coffee mug, then walked into the kitchen to rinse everything off and put them into the dishwasher.   Putting her shoes on and grabbing her purse, she waited on the porch for the car to show up.

Ten minutes later, she was on her way to Alec Brighton's mansion.

*****   *****

Alec and Jose were inside waiting for Eva to arrive. Alec's nerves were shot, and he really wanted to do a line, but was afraid to even move. The gun was still in Jose's hand, which was resting on his lap now and not pointed at him, but he wasn't taking any chances.

Jose felt Alec staring at him, so he gave him a look that made the man flinch. Yep, he still had the power to make people uncomfortable. He took comfort in that. Jose wasn't a pushover by any means.

Alec broke the silence and asked, "you're not going to hurt her, are you?"

The gun came up, and he trained it on the middle of Alec's chest, knowing full well he could easily pull the trigger and not have to listen to this imbecile anymore.

"What I do or don't do to the little witch, is none of your business, Mr. Brighton. You're lucky I don't just take you out right now, but that might upset Jefe."

"Who?"

"Diego Martinez, you idiot."

Jose was getting annoyed by the minute. He needed to end this soon. His life was perfect before Marcella Gallo ruined everything. With that threat taken care of, he assumed he was in the clear. As far as he knew, all that was left of her was her skeleton. He wouldn't have left any trace evidence on that, and even if he had, the acid combined with her sitting at the bottom of Lake Lanier should have taken care of any residual residue.

Alec heard the faint sound of a car door shutting, and panic sliced through him, like a knife. This woman did nothing to warrant what she was coming into here.

Jose heard the door, too. A wicked smile drew across his face as he stood. Turning his attention to Alec he stated in a low voice, "go let her in and don't say a word about my presence. If I hear one word of warning out of you, I'll shoot you both."

Alec walked down the hallway to the foyer and waited until she rang the doorbell. His hand reached out for the handle, and it was shaking from fear. Opening the door, she stood on the stoop with a smile on her pretty face, completely oblivious as to what was about to happen.

"Hi Mr. Brighton, I'm here to meet Agent Long, but I don't see his rental car. Did he leave?"

That's when Alec saw the late model sedan parked on the street in front of his house. He assumed it belonged to the man in his house right now.

Eva took in his silence and waved a hand in front of him, since he seemed a bit out of it. "Mr. Brighton?"

Alec was startled out of his thoughts, "sorry um, Agent Long drove here with one of the detectives." He moved to the side and motioned for her to come in. "Please, come in."

She heard the distinct words emanating from his thoughts, *"Jesus, I wish she wouldn't have come. This is going to end badly."*

"What's going to end badly?"

Alec's eyes went wide. "It's true… You're a witch?"

Her eyes grew larger, as she failed to keep what she heard to herself.

Eva ignored his glaring eyes and followed him down the long hallway. She stopped dead in her tracks when she got to the main great room, when she saw that there was a man standing in the middle of it, glaring at her and holding a gun in his hand. For the moment, it was pointed at the floor and not at her.

"Eva, it is a pleasure to finally meet a real "Bruja", in person."

She noticed the accent and also got his reference. This man knew she was a witch. Upon taking a better look at the man's face, she stepped back one step and bumped into Alec. Turning around, she asked "what's going on here, where is agent Long?"

Before Alec could say a word, Jose moved into her personal space and Eva's hands went up in a defensive stance, "don't touch me," she yelled.

Jose took a pair of zip ties out of his pocket, and in a flash he had one of her hand's, then spun her around, grabbing both wrists tightly, and proceeded to immobilize her.

Panic shot straight through her core. "What is going on?"

"What's going on is, you know and see too much for your own good."

"I still don't know what you're talking about. I don't even know you." She figured if she kept talking and asking questions, the longer she had before something bad happened.

"Chica, I saw you last night in the lake." He let that statement hang in the air for a minute. And then he saw the moment everything clicked into place. "Is it coming back to you now?"

Eva's thoughts were all over the place, wondering how this guy saw her at the lake last night. His face looks like the man from the boat, the one who pulled Marcella out of the water, then a couple of days later, dumped her bones back in. But how does he know that she saw that? He called me Bruja. He knows I'm a witch. Think Eva, think. Stall him, keep talking, do whatever you can to find out more.

"How did you see me last night?"

"Drones are an amazing technological gift for engineers. You see, I'd been following Mr. Alec here and saw that you were all heading out onto the water, and I merely went to the other side of the lake, set my drone up to take off and flew it around the lake until I saw his boat anchor.

I'm sure you expected some modicum of privacy since you went out at night, but that's the beauty of these new drones that have night vision capability, they run on infrared and I didn't have to have any light emanating from it, to see you all on my screen. And since the boat's engines are notoriously loud, there was no chance that any of you would hear it either.

I saw and heard everything. And before anyone finds out my identity, you will be coming with me, and you're going to help me get out of the country.

And one last thing...when I say I saw and heard everything, I mean I saw what you did under the water. Your flashlight that was attached to your mask does not make the kind of light that I saw and the water doesn't move like it did either. I will expose you for what you are."

This guy is certifiable at best, Eva thought, but he did seem to have the upper hand at the moment, and that's never good, in her book.

"What do you want from me?"

Jose grabbed her by the arm and dragged her toward the front door. Once he opened it, she spotted the plainclothes cop sitting across the street, in his unmarked car. A feeling of hope caught in her throat.

"He's not going to help you dear. He actually works for Martinez, as do a lot more people than you think. I'm talking about cops, judges, federal agents, people in the prosecutor's office; you name it, his hands are in their pockets."

A feeling of hopelessness stabbed her in her stomach, when he opened the trunk of his car and pushed her inside. He slammed the trunk shut, and she heard him saying something to Alec, who must have been close by, but she couldn't make out what they were saying.

A door shut and the sound of the engine catching tore her away from her thoughts. Where was he going to take her? Would they ever find her before he killed her, and dumped her remains into the lake? All these questions began swirling around in her mind.

Chapter Forty-two

Kris was in a meeting when his phone alerted him to a text message. When he looked down and read it, all color drained from his face. He got up from the chair he was sitting in and left the room, without saying a word.

He dialed Jake's number and he immediately answered. "Hey, did you guys go somewhere? I just got back to the cabin, and neither of you were here."

"I'm at the office. Eva isn't there anywhere?" His voice cracked on the last word.

There was silence on Jake's end, but Kris could hear doors opening and closing, like he was raiding the house. "She's nowhere around this house, or outside. Would she go hiking on her own, in a new place?"

"No, not if she hasn't been on the trail one or two times prior. Where the hell could she be Jake?"

Jake racked his brain for any ideas as to where she could have gone on our own, but nothing was coming to him. Their cabin was out of the way from any big city. Something came to Jake's mind. "Kris, does she still have the new tracking device on her?"

Kris whipped his laptop open and brought up the app that had the tracking software on it. He logged himself in and saw the blip on the screen moving. "She must be wearing the bracelet, because she's on the move."

"What's the location," Jake asked, as he sprinted toward the car.

"It looks like South of Atlanta somewhere, close to Grove Park."

Kris heard the expletive Jake muttered. "What? What's wrong with that area?"

"It's a pretty bad part of the city. It's littered with gangs, drugs and the homeless. There is on average, two murders every day in that section of Atlanta.

Kris didn't hear everything Jake was saying, because he noticed that the blip stopped moving. He zoomed in to see where it stopped. "Jake, she's stopped."

"Where? Give me the cross streets."

"I can do you one better, I can give you the actual location. The blip stopped at a place called Junk for money, off of Astor Road."

Jake slammed his hand against the steering wheel, and let out a slew of curses.

"Damn it, I know who has her."

"Who took Eva? Tell me!" Kris was yelling through the phone and people were staring at him from their desks. "I'm leaving the office, and I'll be en route."

"I'd rather you stay where you're at."

"Who took my wife, Jake?"

"We just got the name off of the boat registration we saw last night. He's a Mexican national, with some family still living in Juarez. He owns the

Junkyard you just mentioned, as well as an automotive repair shop. His name is Jose Vergera. I already have men on their way to Vergera's home, and they'll bring in his wife if she's there.

We need to get a DNA sample from him to prove he is the one who killed Marcella, but I'm about ninety-nine percent sure he's our guy."

Kris swore under his breath. "How far are you from the junkyard?"

"I'm twenty minutes out."

"I'm heading that way Jake, and you can't stop me," Kris disconnected the call and grabbed his stuff. He ran through the halls to the elevator, willing it to get there quicker.

The elevator dinged and the doors opened. He got in before people were able to get off, and they were now giving him dirty looks, but he ignored them and pushed the first floor button about ten times before the doors started to close. "Come on, hurry up. Can't this thing go any faster?"

He knew he was being unreasonable, but all reason left him the moment he found out Eva had been taken.

Chapter Forty-three

The smooth pavement turned into rolling over gravel, and hitting what felt like bigger rocks. Every single time the car drove over a big rock, Eva bounced around in the trunk. Bruises were forming already on her arms, she could feel it.

Eva felt sweat drip into her eyes and slide down her back. Breathing was starting to get hard, from the stifling heat of being in the trunk with little ventilation.

The car came to a stop and a wave of nausea rolled through her. If the car stopped, it meant they were at their destination. "Oh crap. Gram, a little help here, if you can hear me.

Great, now I'm trying to materialize a dead person."

She could barely feel her fingers, from the zip ties being too tight. Still, she tried pulling at the restraints, only to feel the hard plastic cut through her skin. When she relaxed her hands, she began flexing her fingers to generate some feeling back into them. Her one index finger brushed the other hand, and she felt something on her ring finger. It was her Grandmother's protection ring.

"I'm wearing your ring Gram, but with my hands restrained, there's not much I can do with it.

Figures, the maniac would put my hands behind my back, instead of in the front."

Jose yanked the trunk open and grabbed her by the elbow, pulling her. "Move! I don't have all day."

Eva cried out when he dragged her body over the rough edges of the metal framing of the trunk.

He got her into a standing position and walked her to a dilapidated barn. When he opened the sliding barn door, the smell of oil, gasoline and battery acid assaulted her senses, and she dry-heaved. "Stand up straight," he yelled.

Jose jerked her forward, making her lose her balance, but once she righted herself, she started to take in her surroundings. The barn had a dirt floor that was covered with car parts, military supplies, shells of cars and trucks, old rusted out farm tools, and large metal drums.

He stopped in front of one of the metal drums labeled gasoline . He snatched the lid off of the drum and ordered her to climb inside. Eva resisted by kicking out, and then trying to back away quickly, but he came at her and bent down, grabbing her around the legs, picking her up. He walked over to the open drum and placed her inside.

Her panic was in full swing now. "You can't put me in this thing, I'll suffocate."

"I don't care," was his only response.

He proceeded to pick up the lid to the drum and pushed her head down, so she was basically folding in on herself. She squatted down into the metal container, looking up into his eyes as he put the lid in place. In the empty recesses of his eyes, she saw nothing but darkness. His eyes were black as pitch and held zero remorse.

Eva decided that she was not going to go quietly. She moved around as much as she could in the tight cylinder, and the noise from her feet kicking the sides of the drum echoed loudly . If anything, she thought it would annoy him so much, he'd open the lid, and she could catch a breath. Of course, he could also decide she was useless and get rid of her.

Jose put the palms of his hands to his eyes and rubbed them. The noise echoed throughout the whole barn and even outside it. His thoughts began leaning toward just shooting her on the spot, but her usefulness threw out that option, for the moment.

"Lady, you can make all the noise you want, you'll use up whatever oxygen that is left in there, and you won't be my problem anymore."

She heard him yelling over her kicking, and she stopped. Losing what oxygen she did have would be bad.

Outside the sound of tires rolling over the gravel caught both of their attentions.

"Keep quiet, or I'll shoot whoever is out there," he said in a low voice, next to the drum.

She stayed quiet, but it was mostly so she could hear what or who was out there. The sound of the barn door sliding back into place put her on high alert.

*****   *****

Jake found the entrance to the junkyard and slowed his speed to a crawl. The gravel wasn't helping to keep his arrival secret, so he drove at a snail's pace down the long drive, towards the middle of the junkyard.

A couple of buildings came into view. One looked like it could be the office, with its cement exterior, one door and overhang with the company name on it. The opposite side of the drive, sat a shabby barn that was in need of a lot of repairs.

A figure appeared from inside the barn, and took off for the heaps of junk that spread out over a great expanse of land. Jake saw the gun in the man's hand and came to a screeching halt, putting the car in park and jumping out with his gun in hand. Jake took a shooter's stance and yelled, "Stop!"

The man turned and took a shot at Jake, then kept running.

*****   *****

Eva thought she heard a man yell something but it was muffled, then a gunshot rang out, and she flinched.

"Screw it, I'm not going to die in this stinky barrel."

She began yelling as loud as she could, and kicked at the metal, making as much noise as she possibly could.

"Help, I'm in here! Is someone out there?"

*****   *****

Jake ran to the barn, where the man fled from. He had to check to see if Eva was in there. Jerking the barn door to the side, he heard a clanging of metal and then the most wonderful sound reverberated off the metal.

"Eva!"

"Jake? Jake, I'm in here, one the metal drums. Hurry!"

"Keep hitting the side of the metal, so I can figure out which one you're in."

She did as she was told, and in a matter of seconds, the lid was wrench off the drum. Eva looked up and squinted from the light now streaming in, but she made out Jake's form looking down at her.

"I'm so glad to see you," she said through the tears falling down her cheeks.

He put his hands under her arms and lifted her out, not letting go of her for a minute while she caught her breath. "Are you okay," he asked, taking in her appearance, when he noticed the blood stains in multiple places. Rage was at the forefront of his mind seeing her bleeding. "Where are you hurt?"

"I'm fine, just bruises and small cuts from the trunk of the car."

She spun around quickly, showing him the zip ties. " Get these off of me."

Jake looked around for any kind of tool that would work to rid her of the restraints. He saw the blood and the cuts from her trying to get them off, herself, and he cringed internally. He spotted a pair of pliers and went to work on cutting her free.

"Oh my gosh, thank you," she said, as she shook her wrists, and flexed her fingers.

"Eva, I have to go find Jose. He ran out of here, like a bat out of hell. Luckily this is the first place I ran to, to look for you, but he is out in the junkyard somewhere. You stay here or go to the rental car, lock the doors and stay down below window level, okay?"

She nodded and walked out the door, and Jake took off at a sprint toward the junk.

*****   *****

Kris was sitting in traffic on I-75 driving toward the South side of the city, growing more and more anxious, and angry. "Why did I agree to let her work with Jake?" He cursed himself a blue streak thinking of what he may find once he gets to the junkyard. His GPS showed that he was still a good eight miles away.

He picked up his phone and hit the speed dial to get Jake on the phone, to see if he made it there yet. The phone kept ringing and ringing before it went to voicemail. "Damn it," he said, hitting the steering wheel with the palm of his hand.

"God, I'm going to go out on a limb here, asking, no, begging you, to please keep my Eva safe. I can't lose her, she is my whole world."

*****   *****

Jake ran through piles of flattened cars, bumpers, exhaust pipes, you name it, it was piled high on either side of him. He looked below cars for feet, he opened beat up buses, searching for Jose.

"Jose, give it up, you're not leaving here," Jake yelled out.

Shuffling of feet running through dirt and gravel, pointed Jake in the direction Jose had been holed up. He ran toward the sound, but didn't see anything. His gun held straight out, his body turning from side to side, looking in, under and around the massive amounts of crap. Jake kept a defensive position and made his way along the path.

A slight sound of footsteps caught his attention, but they weren't on the gravel. Jake looked up just as Jose jumped off of a twenty-foot pile of car parts, and landed knocking Jake off balance. The gun in Jose's hand fell to the ground and went off, making the bullet ricochet off the side of a bus.

Jose got to his feet quickly and went after Jake. He had his hand on Jake's arm that held the gun, and the two men went to the ground, each trying to gain a leg up on controlling where the gun pointed.

***** *****

Another gunshot rang out and Eva jumped up from the floor of the car, looking all around her. She saw nothing, but opened the car door, and ran toward the area that Jake had run to.

"This is like a freaking maze," she said under her breath.

She heard a scuffle in the distance and followed the noise. There was a lot of grunting and moaning as she got closer, then everything went dead silent. Eva stopped briefly to listen, but didn't hear anything. She rounded a broken down, rusted out school bus and stopped in her tracks.

The man that kidnapped her had a gun pointed at Jake. Her breath hitched, but Jose didn't seem to notice, however, Jake did, and he gave her an imperceptible nod, telling her not to move or engage.

"As soon as I take care of you amigo, I'm ending the Bruja's life. She can make it so I lose everything, and I can't have that."

"Jose, you don't want to do this. I know Diego Martinez holds your family in Juarez over your head. If you make it out of here alive, he will have you killed elsewhere, and you know that."

"No! I take care of his messes, and do as I'm told. He is a bigger coward than you think."

"Did you take care of a mess of his twenty years ago, too?" Jake didn't have any DNA from him yet to know the truth, but he figured while he was talking, he'd see how he responds.

Jose took a step closer to Jake, held the gun stiffer, aiming right at center mass. "I'm done talking."

Eva stood with her shoulders back, with her fear and anger fueling her. She fisted both hands and pulled all of her energy into them. The light beginning to seep out of them, was just the beginning. Eva screamed at the top of her lungs,

"NOOOOOOOOO!" Her hands flew straight out and the white light shot out of them, going right into the back of Jose's body, sending him flying into the air. Jake dove in the opposite direction grabbing for the other gun and rolling up to his feet.

Jose came down with a loud blood curdling thud, landing on an exhaust pipe that had been cut. The sharpness from the jagged edges and the velocity of his body landing, had the pipe ripping right through his torso.

Jake went to check to make sure that Jose was indeed gone, before he headed in Eva's direction.

Eva dropped to her knees, her whole body trembling and staring at her arms. Jake knelt in front of her, taking her in his arms. "It's over, Eva." She pulled back to look at him, "he's dead?" He nodded, "Oh yeah, he's gone."

Jake felt her body jerk, and she dropped her head to his chest. "Eva, don't you dare be upset about him being dead. You saved my life, and you caught Marcella's killer."

She sniffled back some tears. She knew he was right, she saved his life and got justice for Marcella.

"Holy shit!"

They both turned, and saw Kris staring at the body of Jose Vergera.

Eva ran to him, and wrapped her arms around him, "I can explain," she said.

Kris pulled her back slightly, so he could see her face. "What do you mean you can explain?"

Jake interrupted her before she said anything. "She saved my life, man."

Eva turned her head toward Jake, and gave him a small smile that didn't quite reach her eyes, as it usually did, but he saw the gratitude in them.

That was their silent agreement that Kris didn't always need to know all the specifics.

Chapter Forty-four
Two Weeks Later, back in Ohio

Eva was taping up boxes that she had just finished filling with dishes and glasses from the kitchen cabinets, when the doorbell rang.

She got to the front door and opened it to see Jake standing on her front porch, dressed in jeans and a t-shirt. "Wow, slumming it today, huh?"

He laughed as he entered the house, stopping to give her a quick hug. "I'm not on the clock."

She smiled, "so this is the real you, is that it?"

"I like to be comfortable sometimes, give me a break."

"You know I'm just giving you a hard time. So what do we owe the pleasure of this visit? You know I can't help you with any cases for at least a month, since we've got to get the house ready to move."

"Yeah, I know. I still can't believe you're all moving down to Georgia now."

"Blame Kris, the Director of Engineering begged him to move to that office. He said it was an offer he just couldn't pass up.

So, why are you here then, if you don't need my assistance?"

"I wanted to check on you, and also let you know that after Miguel and Juan found out about Jose's unfortunate demise, they sang like a choir, naming Diego Martinez's whole ring. I was kind of surprised at how many Atlanta cops he had under his belt. It was disappointing , to say the least.

Chief Montgomery found out about the one undercover cop that was watching Brighton's house, being merely a spy for Diego, and that ticked him off royally that he didn't see it. He hadn't seen it in any of the guys that were arrested. I felt bad for the guy.

He even had a few judges, a paralegal in the prosecutors office and a few city government workers, as well. But, Diego has since been arrested along with all of his cronies. He'll be going away for a long time. They picked up the Port Authority worker he paid off to get the boats through, too.

So, all in all, this was a successful case, in more ways than one. You did good, Eva."

"What about your case from twenty years ago? Did they get a match to Jose's DNA?"

Jake smiled, "they did."

"You closed the one case that hung over your head for twenty years, congratulations."

"Thanks. The best part though, was giving the family some closure."

"I bet they appreciated that very much."

Eva continued walking them toward the kitchen, "so how about helping us pack?"

He gave her a smug smile, "can't."

"Why not? What do you have to do that's better than this," she waved her arm out over the many boxes, packing paper, and tape that cluttered her kitchen floor.

"I have to pack my place up."

Her mouth dropped open in surprise, and before she could ask, he said, "did you honestly think I'd let you all move to Georgia without me?"

The End

Thank you for reading Lying Lanier, an Eva St. Claire Mystery.

Look for Eva, Jake and Kris' next adventure, when they take on Savannah, Georgia, in Book 4 - Slaying Savannah.

Follow me on Social Media for up to date information on my new books, my podcast and general info.

Website: www.authormkstabley.com

Facebook: @authormkstabley

Instagram: @m.k.stableyauthor

Spotify: @The Talking Book Podcast

Made in the USA
Middletown, DE
06 January 2023